CROSSFIRE

She pushed herself to her feet and leaned back in the doorway, trying to find out where she'd ended up. It didn't seem familiar to her, but nowhere was familiar any more, she'd spent so long just wandering it was all a blur. And her head hurt and her stomach hurt and it was hard just to concentrate. She wished the two boys were with her. But they were gone.

Everything had gone: the address, all the hopes she had, the two boys, her direction and all her cash. There was no place to go but to keep roaming round the streets, to keep watching and hoping and looking out. Looking out for the street gangs and the two boys she hoped she'd find.

Other titles in the Mystery Thriller series include:

CROSSFIRE

Peter Beere

Illustrated by David Wytt

Hippo Books
Scholastic Publications Limited
London

Scholastic Publications Ltd.,
10 Earlham Street, London WC2H 9RX, UK

Scholastic Inc.,
730 Broadway, New York, NY 10003, USA

Scholastic Canada Ltd.,
123 Newkirk Road, Richmond Hill,
Ontario L4C 3G5, Canada

Ashton Scholastic Pty Ltd.,
P O Box 579, Gosford, New South Wales,
Australia

Ashton Scholastic Ltd.,
165 Marua Road, Panmure, Auckland 6,
New Zealand

First published by Scholastic Publications Ltd., 1991

ISBN 0 590 76415 2

Typeset by AKM Associates (UK) Ltd., Southall, London
Printed by Cox and Wyman Ltd., Reading, Berks

Chapter One

The old man leaned forward from his waist, standing
on tiptoe, his nose bent inquisitively, as he scrabbled
about in the bottom of a rubbish bin. His feet almost
left the ground, his legs writhed to drive him deeper,
and he came up ecstatically with a loaf of bread. More
precisely it was half a loaf, wrapped up with old silver
foil, but he clutched it as though he'd found a
treasure trove.

He grunted triumphantly, stuffed the loaf inside
his coat, and bent back to see what other food he'd
find that night. He was having a good night. Sometimes it was much harder, sometimes he found
nothing at all to eat. But he'd already loaded up most
of his many pockets. He could eat like a king. Or a
starving man.

It was a hot night in June but the old man was wrapped up as though he thought blizzards from the Arctic might be on the way. He had so many clothes on it was hard to move about in them. He grunted again, but with strain this time.

One of his belts (he had several) had caught on the edge of the bin, and he had to wriggle himself backwards to get away. This made the old man dizzy, so he rested a while, crouching by the bin. He wasn't as old as he looked; he was about fifty-five, but there were times when he could look about ninety or even older. He had a lot of lines on his face, raw cuts like river valleys, and his eyes had sunk deep in their sockets. It was because of the life he led, a scratching life, scraping for food; he wasn't sure what he looked like, he never looked in a mirror.

The old man sighed without any particular reason, struggled up to his feet and wiped his nose on a long length of coloured rag. Then he went back to the bin again and reached in the heart of it. It was a good night for hunting. He was doing well.

He muttered quietly to himself as he rummaged through all the waste, tossing boxes aside, and pausing to study scraps. Every now and then he found something which looked like it had some use, so he would put that to one side, in a growing heap. He had already picked out a box in which he could take all these treasures away. He thought it must be his birthday. His lucky day.

Something flashed in his hand – a long knife with a bloodstain on – and that puzzled the old man and he stopped for a while. He looked carefully around the street as though someone was watching him, or maybe he was searching for a body. But no one was there. The whole street was deserted. After a moment he went back to work again.

He'd been lucky to find this street, lucky that no other beggars had got there before him. If there'd been other beggars he would have had to *fight* for his treasure trove. That's maybe why he hung on to the knife for a while. But a few moments later, he tossed it to one side; it wasn't his business, he had other things to do. If other folk wanted to fight, that was their problem; as far as he was concerned they could just get on with it. But from time to time he looked at the knife, lying there gleaming brightly, and every once in a while he seemed to shake a little.

He began to sing quietly, changed it to a low humming, and then settled for occasional grunted notes. It was hard to hold on to tunes. It was hard just to *think* for long. The old man's mind was liable to wander. But he didn't mind, he'd kind of grown used to it. As long as nobody bothered him he was fine.

He stopped very suddenly, poked up his head and stared down the street. He thought that he had heard something, the soft pad of running feet – for a moment he wished that he'd kept the knife. He didn't need any trouble now with all the good luck he'd had, he didn't want to have to fight in order to protect his trove.

But it was only a young girl, he could see her as she reached the light. Her coat streamed out behind her,

her curls were wild. She was running from something but he couldn't see what it was. There was no one behind her, just an empty street. He wanted to say "You can stop now; it's all right, you're on your own." But she'd passed him by before he had a chance to speak. He could still hear her footsteps in the distance for a long time, it appeared they would never stop. He wondered what must have frightened her to make her take flight like that, like a young lonely animal, sick with fear. There was a lot in these parts for a girl to be frightened of.

There was a lot for old men to be frightened of, he thought, with a sigh.

Perhaps it was nothing, perhaps she stayed out too late. But he didn't think so, from the way she was running. She was running as though something terrible was right behind, and that bothered him so he couldn't relax again. First the girl frightened him, now she'd unsettled him; it wasn't such a good night for him after all.

He gathered up his things, which didn't seem quite so interesting now, dropped them all in the box and tucked it in his coat. It was too big to fit but he bent his arms over it, to shield it, and to save it from prying eyes. You could not trust anyone – they all wanted what you'd got. There'd even be someone who'd fight for junk.

He returned to his room, which was more like a cupboard really; there wasn't enough room to fit a bed inside. But he was lucky to have the place, lucky nobody else had it. He settled down on a mattress which he'd crammed into his room and spread his night's haul out carefully and looked through it. There was plenty to eat, there were things he could read for a while, till the candle gave out and the darkness came. There was even a whistle that he could play an old tune on; one of the old tunes he remembered from way back when he was young.

Could it have really been so long? It was hard to remember now. But he smiled as he thought back to what he'd been. He was considerably happier now. There was no one to hassle him, there was no one to make up his mind for him. It could be hard on the road, there was no doubt of that, it could be hard in the winter months, but he didn't think, on the whole, he had lost too much. He could go where he wanted to go and do what he wanted to do. No, he'd never go back again; he had it made.

So he curled up in a blanket and hummed a tune happily. He was snug, he was well fed, he was warm at heart.

But one thing kept bothering the old man – the girl sprinting along that street. She made him sleep restlessly. He kept wondering just who she was, where she came from and what she'd seen that made her run so hard . . .

The girl finally stopped running. She had run out of fear and steam. She slumped down in a doorway to catch her breath.

The gang had eventually stopped following her, she was practically sure of that, they gave up when she left the bright lights of town. They didn't go in the darkness, they stayed round the city's heart. In the darkness was danger. They hugged the light.

There were lots of gangs on the street, stupid gangs, petty gangs, gangs of youngsters, of kids even, ten years old. They were so young they were laughable, but together they were tough enough. Maybe someone behind them showed them what to do. It didn't matter that you're one of them, a kid trying to survive. You might not have too much, but they wanted it.

Maggie didn't have much, just some clothes and some souvenirs, but that was enough to attract the gang, like a flame. They chased her for miles, they were only dumb little kids, they couldn't even run fast on their stubby legs. But they wanted that bag, they were willing to *hurt* for it. They chased her half-way through London, for a stupid bag.

Maggie put her head in her hands and thought that the next time she'd *give* them the bag, it wasn't worth it for the few things she had in it. Maybe a couple of days earlier she'd have put up a fight for it, but somehow it seemed more important then. Now it was baggage that just slowed her down. Now she could probably dispense with it.

Maybe she ought to dump the thing anyway and make do with what she had; if it brought that much trouble, was it worth the sweat? But she thought she'd hang on to it, at least for a day or two. If they chased her again, they could have the bag.

She pushed herself to her feet and leaned back in

the doorway, trying to find out where she'd ended up. It didn't seem familiar to her, but nowhere was familiar any more; she'd spent so long just wandering it was all a blur. And her head hurt and her stomach hurt and it was hard just to concentrate. She wished the two boys were with her. But they were gone.

Everything had gone: the address, all the hopes she had, the two boys, her direction and all her cash. There was no place to go but to keep roaming round the streets, to keep watching and hoping and looking out. Looking out for the street gangs and the two boys she hoped she'd find. Looking out for some food, or she'd starve to death.

After a moment she swung the bag on to her shoulder and set off on her journey along the street.

She was fourteen years old but you'd never have known it. The streets made her tougher. They made her old.

Chapter Two

The old man went happily into the off-licence; he had 98p and could buy some booze. It wouldn't be much but it would help him to get to sleep. Sometimes he was frightened of his dreams, which were pretty bad.

He hung around for a while for there was nothing much else to do, and checked every single bottle inside the place. He kept an eye on the dog, which didn't like people hanging round. But the dog was half-hearted. It didn't care.

After he'd read every label again for a third time the owner said, "Are you planning on buying something?" He was a tall, ugly man wearing a dirty shirt. His braces could barely reach round his waist.

"Yeah, probably," said the old man. "I'm thinking, I can't decide."

"You try nicking something, I'll set this Alsatian on you."

"Yeah, what a threat!" sneered the old man. "That old dog doesn't frighten me."

"He should do, this dog has been trained to kill."

"Yeah, I believe that," said the old man. "Probably kills you with boredom." He turned his back and returned to the rows of shelves.

While he was doing that he kept counting his money in the hope that he'd got his addition wrong. He hoped that he might have overlooked something and would find some more tucked away, but it didn't matter how often he went through his piles of clothes, he found no more loose coins, just a roll of gum. He was sure that he'd had more and couldn't think what he'd done with it. Maybe he spent it on food, it was hard to say. It was hard to keep track of things with his mind always wandering. Maybe he'd *hidden* it, to keep it safe.

It took him a long while then to try to remember where he might have put something to keep it safe. Maybe inside the mattress? No, he'd hidden stuff there before, and someone found it and nicked it. They always did. But still, he was lucky, they could have stolen the mattress. Maybe he'd hidden it elsewhere. Or maybe not.

By the time he got through thinking, which took quite a while for him, it had grown dark in the streets and the lights were on. This seemed to be happening now, that he'd just drift away for hours. Perhaps I've grown senile? he thought.

But he didn't care. He didn't care about much these days – except that frightened girl was still bothering him, although he might have even dreamed her, he wasn't sure. He was still trying to picture her when the door bell gave one short ring. He turned around. Two young boys had come in the shop.

They were only two kids, they couldn't have been more than sixteen, they couldn't get served in that place, but they probably would. The old man didn't care, all he needed was time alone. He went back through his pockets. But there was no more cash.

He wondered if maybe it was worth trying to ask one of the kids for some, but the tall one was already talking to the owner, trying to get him to reach something that was out of sight.

"What do you want to have that for?" The man glared at the highest shelf. "It's for ladies, can't you settle for something else?"

"No, I want to try that," said the kid, and the owner reached down for a stool, scowling.

He pulled himself wearily up off the ground on to the stool, which wasn't easy with all the spare fat he carried. He swayed around like a spinning-top and threatened to tumble down, but he steadied and reached up, and the smaller boy moved. He jumped up on the counter and grabbed at the nearest shelf, where the spirits were stored safely out of reach. He grabbed a big bottle and fled the scene.

"Hey, you there! Come back with that!" The man started to howl at him. "You come back with that bottle! Go on, get him dog!"

10

The dog bounded to his feet, he was all teeth and dripping jaws. He was growling, and then he ran for the door.

The owner jumped after him. The boy had fled down the street. He flung the door wide and threw the dog at the night. *"Go on, get off after him! Go on, don't just sit there, dog!"* But the dog had given up, and had settled down. The dog didn't like the night, he didn't like going out on his own. He liked being in the shop and lying down. He wasn't really too keen on this business of chasing people. He lay down, yawned, then closed his eyes.

"What do you think I feed you for?" The owner was screaming at the dog. He couldn't believe it. He was apopleptic. He started to run himself.

But the kid had disappeared by then, along with the stolen goods. The owner howled in the street and punched at the dark.

And while all this was going on the other youth sidled out, and the old man helped himself to a box of wine. He tucked it inside his coat and tipped a wink to the yawning dog. Then he sneaked out himself, and went running home.

A hundred yards along the street Gerald dropped the bottle. Liam couldn't believe it, he stared in horror as the amber liquid drained in the gutter and the glass spewed like cats' eyes across the road.

"You've dropped it!" he gasped. "I can't believe it, you've dropped the thing!"

"I couldn't help it," said Gerald. "My hands were damp."

"*Your* hands were damp? What about *my* hands?" Liam yelled at him. "You left me standing there with a fifteen-stone killer dog! And what do you think they're going to say when we say that we dropped it? They'll kick us out, Gerald, we'll be on the streets again!"

"Look!" Gerald stopped and turned round so he faced Liam. "If you're so smart, Liam, go and steal another bottle! *I* took the risks. It was *me* had the dog after him. All you had to do was watch and just walk away."

The two youths were on the brink of a mutual slanging match, they'd never stolen before and it made them scared. Not only were they scared but they'd now gone and ruined it all. So they got angry, and both went into a sulk.

For a long time they walked without looking at one another, giving off clouds of invisible, bitter smoke.

"It's your fault," muttered Liam.

"Oh, go kiss a duck!" said Gerald.

But it didn't bring back the bottle. Their prize was gone.

They didn't need the bottle so they could get themselves drunk on it, they didn't even *like* booze. They had pinched it to pay their way. They had fallen in with other Irish lads who had offered them a bed for the night, though it wasn't so much a bed, it was more like a pile of rags. In return they had to steal something, and their hosts didn't want paper clips, they wanted whisky or cigarettes or even drugs.

Liam and Gerald had no idea at all how to find drugs, so they settled for whisky, but then went and dropped the haul. They had given it to the drains so the rats could go wild on it. It was pretty much the way things had gone for them.

They didn't think they could steal again, their nerves were too shot by now. And they had no cash at all, they had lost all that. They hadn't so much lost it as fed it to slot machines. In fact, everything they did seemed to make things worse.

They had travelled from Ireland to seek out a new life for themselves. What a big joke that looked now. They nearly died laughing.

Chapter Three

An old man was carefully sweeping the dirt up, from the pavements, to the gutters, to his yellow cart. This man really *was* old, he was older than the other man who'd watched Maggie run, saw the shop theft, and who'd grabbed the wine. This man was at least in his seventies, and possibly older. But he never ceased from his sweeping. He loved his work.

He wasn't employed by the Council, nor even the Government, nor by the traders nor shopkeepers whose streets he cleaned. He just worked because he wanted to, because it made him feel happy. He wanted to make Central London clean.

He knew the task was impossible, but at six every morning he pushed out his hand-cart and went to work. He worked through until midnight, occasionally stopping to rest, or to talk or to eat or to stare into space. Everyone round there knew him, they all said hello to him. He lived on handouts, and couldn't have asked for more.

The man loved what he did and he smiled as he cleaned the streets. He sang songs while he worked and he always did his best. He was a proud little man, and he cleaned streets well.

He looked up as a friend approached with a grin on his wrinkled face, and the street-cleaner said, "What's all this then, Tom? You look like you won the pools. Did you finally get lucky?"

The old man beamed. He said, "No, but I'm lucky, Jim. Look what old Tom's got –" And he pulled the front of his coat apart and there was a big box of wine tucked inside his belt. "I've got wine, I've got cake, I've been really in luck this week. Do you want to come round to my place and celebrate?"

"What, to your place?" said the street-cleaner. "The box with a mattress in?"

"Yeah, why not?" said the old man, and the cleaner laughed.

"Yeah, I'm walked off me feet, let's go and kick up some noise, Tommy! We'll have a party like we did in the old days!"

The old man beamed happily because it *had* been a better week. Except for that girl, and he was starting to forget her now.

While the old men were walking through the streets round to Tom's place, Maggie had found a spot where she could rest for the night. It was an old wooden lean-to at the back of a grocer's shop. It was packed out with boxes, and smelled of fruit.

She made up a rough bed by unfolding some boxes and flattening them out, and then huddled down. It was quiet, but there were rustlings of mice in the latticed roof, and the wind made a sound like the barn back home. It took her a long time to settle because there was a dog howling somewhere, like a fox in the woods round the fields at home. Foxes kept her awake at night with their maniacal screaming; this wild dog in London was doing the same.

There was also a cat nearby which was wailing pathetically, like her own cat in Ireland, a ginger tom. He made a noise like a thrush being strangled. He scratched at the windows to be let in.

Altogether the night played a strange kind of symphony, as if the city came alive with nocturnal life. It all seemed out of place, as if the city held secrets of things that the people didn't know about. Because there weren't any people around, just the sound of their growling cars. It seemed that at night the city belonged to another world.

It wasn't the world Maggie had thought it would be when she first planned to run away; it was considerably different from all her dreams. In her dreams it was magical, the streets were of solid gold. But they weren't made of gold. They were paving stones.

Though this didn't prevent her from still having dreams to fill – if she found the two boys it could

16

change again. That's where it went wrong, when the two boys got yanked away, and she still didn't know where they had gone. But Maggie was young and she had a great many dreams. In the morning she'd try to fulfil them again.

She went to sleep as the dog howled, and the rats rustled.

The old men slept too, side by side on their little bed. And their snores were like growling. Only twice as loud.

Chapter Four

"You know, I had a strange dream last night," the old man told the street-cleaner. "About a young girl I saw a few days ago. She was running down the street and these creatures were after her, and she was all dressed in white, and she sprouted wings. And then I thought – no, she's not a girl, it's like she's a *street*-angel." He shifted nervously. "Do you ever get dreams like that, Jimmy?"

The street-cleaner grunted. They'd spent the night on the mattress and his body had seized up and filled with cramp. He said, "I've been here twelve years, Tom, and I've seen just about everything. Yeah, sometimes I think I see angels too."

"You do?" The old man grunted. "I thought it was just me," he said.

"No, there's all kinds of things, Tom. There's angels, too."

The old man kept thinking about the white street-angel. Where did she come from? And where was she running to?

Maggie didn't feel like an angel, she felt like a heap of rags. But her clothes smelled of apples, and that was good. It was better than the dirt that she'd slowly accumulated, the smell of car fumes and fast food and grimy clothes.

If she'd been back in Ireland she could have walked out the cottage door and the wind would have swept her with morning dew. She would have smelled like the heather, like the green fields and lazy sheep. She would have smelled like the sea, which was close at hand.

She had lost quite a lot it seemed, but she never regretted it. She was quietly determined to see this through. And the first thing to do was to find where her aunty lived. That was the first thing to do, after finding food.

This was a problem for Maggie as she wasn't a pushy girl, and she couldn't find it within her to beg for food. And she hadn't quite got so low that she'd pick up discarded food. All the same, she was hungry. She could eat a cow.

She shouldered her bag and slipped on to the city streets. But before twenty yards passed, Maggie had a fright. There was a girl sprawled in front of her as if she'd been hit by a speeding truck. She looked pole-axed. She looked like she'd never move.

"Are you all right?" whispered Maggie.

"Oh yeah, I just had a sleep. I get these dizzy spells, I have to lie down for a while."

"But you're lying in the *street*," said Maggie.

"I know, I've just got no class." The girl stood up and grinned. "I get stiff as owt." She had a broad northern accent, she had come down from Sunderland. "You aren't weighed down with food in that bag I suppose?"

"No, I've got nothing."

"That figures." The girl looked around. "Never mind, we'll soon get something. We'll clean a few kitchens out, that's usually good for something. They never pay out any money though."

"Am I coming too?" said Maggie.

"What do you want to do, hang around here? I'll do the washing, you can dry – then we've got it made!" And the girl stuck her hand out. "I'm Karen. Are you Irish?"

"Why, do I sound like it?"

"Oh no, Queen of England, kid!" The girl hooted delightedly. "You smell like a bag of peat! Welcome to London, you poor helpless thing!" And she laughed as she led Maggie down the street.

The two boys were nervous. The room they'd been living in was hardly palatial, but it was better than living in egg boxes. And now they were certain they were about to be bundled out. They had turned up with nothing, and the boss was bored.

The boss was called Murphy, and he was several years older than them. Murphy was king of the squat that the boys had found. There were seven youths in the place and all of them were Irish. Murphy demanded they all pay their proper way.

"So why not?" he said. "Don't take much to rob off-licences."

"Well, we had some, but then Liam dropped it," said Gerald.

Liam was mortified. "*I* didn't drop it!" he said. "It was you went and dropped it, *you* mucked it up!"

"So you wasted good booze," said Murphy, interrupting the argument, staring off idly into the blue. "That's pretty bad, boys. That's pretty dumb really. This place don't run on charity you know, we all pull our weight in here. I mean, *I* took you in. Took you off the streets –"

"I know," mumbled Gerald, and his eyes stared down at his feet. "We're very grateful."

"I know you are, but here's the point. See –" Murphy chewed on a matchstick. "I am not like a – what's the word? I'm not a *philanthroper*, I'm more like a businessman. Do you get what I'm saying, boys?"

The two boys said nothing, but both of them bowed their heads sombrely.

"This is my little empire and I rule the roost in here, and while I've got the say of things, that's how it is. Either you cough your rent up or you're out on the street, boyos. Unless you think –" he paused to spit the chewed matchstick out. "You could maybe think how's you'd like to make a few changes, like – let's say you wanted to take control. You could maybe have better ideas, so you come and see me about it, and then you say how you'd like to see things arranged. Then I beat your brains out and we sit down and talk about it. And then we go back to the previous way." His blue eyes looked challengingly from beneath a great mat of hair. "Do you get what I'm saying, boys? *Go and steal some stuff!*"

Then his face found a smile and he nudged them encouragingly. "Just go out there and see what you've got to do. There's a whole city out there. It's London, you've got it made! There are more shops out there than we've cows back home! Go on out and just get something!" His arms spread expansively. "I'm a generous man, I would *like* you to stay right here! But you've got to pay your way, boys, you can't hang on Mummy now. Go on out, be men! Go and *steal* something!"

Gerald smiled nervously. "Well, we'll both do our best," he said.

"I *know* you will!" Murphy clapped them both on the back.

"I don't think I can do it, Gerald."

"Do what?"

"Go and steal something."

"Why not?"

"I just can't, I'm not made that way. I mean, *you* go and steal something, I'll find somewhere else to stay. I'll sleep rough. Or maybe I'll sleep in the park."

"Don't be daft, you'll get killed, Liam. Stay at the squat with me."

"I don't want to."

"That's the problem. Nor do I," said Gerald.

"Are *you* going to steal something?"

"I don't know. What do you think?"

"It's up to you."

"I don't think I can do it either, Liam."

"So what are we going to do then? All our stuff's there –"

"We'll sneak it out."

"We could leave it there." There was a pause.

"Aye, that might be best. Maybe we'd better just leave it there."

So they went down to Piccadilly and watched as the crowds flowed by. The street-cleaner swept by and winked his eye.

Liam said, after thinking for a while, "Do you think maybe we made a mistake, Gerald?"

Gerald thought about it. "I don't think so. Do *you* think we did?"

Liam shrugged. "I don't know," he said. "I wonder how Maggie is."

"Or *where* Maggie is." Gerald gave a sigh.

Chapter Five

Karen was smart. Karen had been around. Karen knew just about everything. She knew places to stay, the places to scavenge for food, and the places to keep well away from. She was sixteen years old and she'd lived rough for eighteen months. Karen thought she knew it all. Maggie hoped she did.

They got breakfast that morning by cleaning a yard out, and the owner said, "You can call back this evening."

"Are we going to go back?" said Maggie.

"Maybe." Karen merely shrugged. "We'll see how we feel. Something else might come up."

"He seemed a nice man."

"Yeah, they're usually the worst," said Karen. "These days you just don't trust anyone. That's the first rule to learn, Maggie; *we're all on our own out here*. You don't put too much faith in anybody."

This was a difficult rule for Maggie to understand, brought up as she was in a small Irish town where you never locked your doors at night and the postman would come in and put the kettle on. Maggie was accustomed to trusting people. She might have been scared of a few of them, but inside she still tried to believe in them.

"There must be a few good people."

"Oh sure, and some right nutters, and you can't tell them apart, you remember that." Karen was very much the older girl, taking Maggie under her wing. She would see her right.

"See, like we say back in Sunderland 'there's nowt comes for nowt no more'. You've got to remember that, or you're never going to learn to survive."

"But I don't want to just *survive*," said Maggie. "I want to try to have a nice life."

"Ha!" Karen laughed. "So why did you come down to London then?"

But Maggie didn't say anything. Her reasons were secret still. She wasn't sure that she understood them herself properly.

"Hey, Tom! How you doing?" yelled Karen, startling Maggie's reverie. She looked around, and saw the old man looking at them.

He'd been startled too, for a moment, but now he was grinning at them. "Oh, it's you, Karen! Oh, you know, doing fine, I'm okay, you know. I've been through a lucky streak." Then the old man peered

25

closer. "Hey, I've seen your friend there before, you know. Did you know she's an angel? Did you know that? A regular street-angel."

"Yeah, she's sure pretty cute!" laughed Karen, and she steered Maggie through a door. "Looks like you've already picked up a fan, Maggie."

But Maggie didn't say anything, for she suddenly found herself in a department store that looked bigger than her home town. It was so big it looked like you could probably get lost in it. It was so big she thought they should lay a trail.

"What are we doing in here, Karen?" she whispered.

"I've got to steal a new lawn-mower."

"*A what*?"

"I'm just kidding. Stick with me, baby."

Karen led the way up a flight of rarely used service stairs and flung open a door, with a sweeping bow. "Behold!" she said dramatically. "A place for the angels! Feast your green eyes and weep, this is home, baby!"

"Gerald, my feet hurt."

"Will you shut up your moaning, Liam! You know, you haven't stopped moaning since we got off the boat."

"Well they do hurt, I'm not kidding, I think I've got blisters coming. Look at them –" Liam stopped to untie his boots.

"Look, I don't want to look at your feet! Leave

26

your boots alone will you. If they're that bad you'll never get them on again."

"Oh why did we come, Gerald?" Liam groaned like a pining dog.

"Because the tooth fairy brought us, why d'you *think*, Liam?"

Gerald was starting to get mad. Gerald wanted to dump Liam, but if he did he'd be totally on his own. He might be big in Dromiskin but here he was out of his depth. And it was no place for drowning, he'd learned that much.

"Where are we going now?" moaned Liam.

"How do *I* know, shut up will you! Go and walk over there, on the other side!"

So that's how they walked, along opposite pavements. Anybody watching would have thought that they'd lost their minds, because Liam kept waving and Gerald kept sticking two fingers up.

They had a long-distance argument, which Liam won.

"Is this where you live?" said Maggie.

"Only in the daytime. I don't push my luck, I clear out at night." Karen threw herself down on a bundle of carpet tiles and magnanimously offered Maggie the open floor. "There's no one comes in here much, it's just an old store-room, but it keeps you out of the rain and you can get some kip. You have to be quiet like, 'cause the store-snoopers sniff you out. I got caught in here once, but I just threw up."

"*You threw up?*" said Maggie.

"Yeah, it works every time. You throw up, and they forget what they nabbed you for. Of course, you have to keep practising, I mean, it's not easy throwing up. Not to order. You've got to have – like a cue."

"What kind of a cue?" said Maggie.

"Well, something to trigger you off. Like, say, what I'd do, I'd think about *you* throwing up. I mean, nobody wants to see somebody puking up, so you think about that, then you just throw up."

"But doesn't it make you sick?"

Karen groaned, and she rolled her eyes. "Well of course it does, that's the whole point of it! There wouldn't be *any* point if you swallowed it down again!"

Maggie gave it some thought. "I don't think I could do it."

"You could if you tried hard enough. It's got me out of some pretty tough spots, you know. You want to think about it, you really want to try it, kid."

Maggie still seemed doubtful and hoped they'd soon change the subject. She just hoped she wasn't sitting down where Karen puked.

She looked round the room, which was small, bare and basic, but, like Karen said, it was somewhere to rest your head. There were a few wire display stands and the carpet tiles Karen sat on, and a few little knick-knacks that Karen had brought in. They were mostly cosmetics, with some scent bottles, a broken mirror, a Mel Gibson poster, and a pile of clothes.

"Are these your clothes?" said Maggie.

"Yeah, you can put a few on if you like. It don't

matter much, I mostly just nick them all. That skirt is good –" and she reached for a leather skirt. "Just try that on, it looks like it'll suit you."

"It's a bit short," said Maggie.

"Yeah well, that's the style, innit? Go on, try that, and put that pink top with it. Go on, put that pink top on, and then put this necklace round, and – where've I gone and put all that make-up now?" Karen looked round excitedly. She was really getting into this, and Maggie was caught up in the enthusiasm. "And try this on, Maggie!"

Ten minutes later, Maggie looked like some kind of a street-walker.

"I'm getting hungry, Gerald."

"Well chew on a brick, Liam."

"And I think, I think maybe I'm hyper-tense."

"You're getting *me* hyper-tense, Liam! Give me a break will you? How can I think while you keep rabbiting on all the time?"

There was a moment of silence, then Liam coughed nervously. "What are you thinking *about*, Gerald?"

Gerald sighed. He let his dark brown eyes roll slowly heavenwards. He said, "I'm trying to think how to get rid of *you*, Liam!"

"Get rid of *me*?" said Liam. "What have I done, what's wrong with me? What do you keep picking on me for, I'm your friend, Gerald."

Gerald sighed bitterly. "Yeah, which just goes to show that I'm even unlucky in the friends I get. You'd think that maybe just once I could have a bit of *good* luck!" Which made Liam disconsolate, and he wanted to cry for a while.

"Why do you hate me, Gerald?"

"Because you're just *there*, Liam!" Gerald started to walk faster to shake him off.

But Liam stuck to his heels like a dog to its master. And they walked around London in single file.

If they hadn't been hurrying so much they might have seen somebody watching them, someone who chewed on a broken match and sneered at them.

Chapter Six

The old man was glad that the new girl had found a friend. She'd be safe enough with Karen. He liked Karen.

He liked quite a few of the youngsters that he met on his travels, but too many of them were sullen and didn't want to talk. He liked passing the time with people when he was in the mood for it. He'd pass the time of day with anyone, especially kids. The kids were more lively, they had a lot more to talk about; as they got older it seemed they had less and less to say. The older they got the more introverted they became, until by the time they got to his age they were all talked out. Then they usually found new friends that came out of paper bags; they could spend their whole lives with their bottles of booze. They'd even drink

31

diesel oil, he'd known people knock that back. They'd drink anything if it helped pass some time away.

The youngsters, he'd noticed, were drinking a lot more these days; and glue sniffing, they went in for that, too. He'd tried it himself once but it wasn't too successful, he practically blew his mind with it. But he didn't blow it for good reasons, he was practically hospitalized. He stuck his head in the bag too far and swallowed glue. A mouthful of Evo Stik. His teeth ached for a fortnight. He'd just tried it once, which was quite enough.

But the booze, that was different, it was a dangerous friend to know, it was so easy to let it just trickle down. And it didn't bring any answers, he'd talked to it often enough to know. It just kept asking questions. He mistrusted booze.

In fact he steered clear of most things because they weren't really necessary; as long as you liked your own company you could get along. He thought that was the problem with a lot of the folks around these days; they didn't like their own company, so they turned to booze. They didn't like themselves much and thought it was helping them, when all they were doing was trying to punish themselves. Booze was for losers, he was pretty sure of that. It was one of the few things he had an opinion on.

Aye, the number of young people who were roaming the streets these days. He shook his head; it wasn't like that in the early days. When *he* hit the road, which must have been thirty years ago, it was mostly old sailors and folk like that. People who drifted without any proper roots. But now, anybody could join the road.

He didn't know why, whether it was boredom or lack of help, or a chance to escape from some awful life. But could the world be so bad that the street-life was better? He had no answers, but the question kept bothering him.

They said there were three thousand people living rough on the city's streets these days. That was bigger than some towns that he'd travelled through.

They were in a park, looking at a pelican, when Karen said, "Where are you from, Maggie?"

Maggie considered. Not because she didn't know, but she didn't know if she was ready to talk about this. If she started letting secrets out would it make life more difficult? And once she started, would she ever know where to stop?

She scraped her heels on the ground. A pigeon flew down at the sound, as if it thought she was offering some food. But they had no food left. They'd eaten their hamburgers and the boxes were empty beside them now.

She wished that she'd kept something to offer the pigeon, but in fact the bird wasn't that bothered by it. It was better fed than she was. It was so stuffed with sliced bread it could barely get its belly to clear the ground. But the bird knew life is tough and you eat every chance you get. Maggie was learning that, too. It was Lesson Two.

Karen was looking away absently, watching the

pelican. Maggie studied her profile. She liked Karen. If there were more people like Karen around then life wouldn't be so difficult. But Karen had her own problems, or she wouldn't be here.

Maggie cleared her throat carefully. "I come from Dromiskin," she said. "It's a little town about twelve miles from the border. It's not far from Dublin, we used to go on the train sometimes. We all lived on a farm. We kept milk cattle."

"A farm?" Karen looked around. "That sounds pretty good," she said.

"It's okay I guess. I suppose you get used to it. It got a bit quiet sometimes."

"Who did you live there with? Your mum and dad?"

Maggie hesitated. "My real parents are dead," she said quietly. "I lived with my stepfather."

"Oh yeah," Karen nodded her head. "The typical story, there's loads of kids round here run away like that."

"No, it wasn't like that," said Maggie. "He always looked after me. It's just –" she stopped. What exactly was it she was trying to say?

She lived on a farm in the depths of the countryside and from one of the hills you could see Dublin Bay, and when the wind was in the right direction you could smell the sea. The grass was so green it could hurt your eyes to look at it and it was sometimes so deep that sheep got lost in it. There was the smell of the sea – and when she closed her eyes she could practically smell it again.

The wind rustled by; like the traffic it never stopped. She looked around. This was hardly real grass at all. The park was covered in rubbish and fat, bloated pigeons. They wouldn't last for five minutes on the hills back home, on the hills where the falcons soared. For a moment she saw them fly, and she trembled as the memories washed over her.

It had been fine for a time when they first moved into the farm, when her mother had been married to Patrick Brady. Her own father died when Maggie was only a little girl, and for a few years after that they had run a store. It was just a small general store, they would never get rich from it. One day her mother sold it, and moved them both into town.

Then she worked in a bar for a while, and it was there that she met Patrick Brady. He was big in the town. They didn't know why then.

After a time they got married and moved to the peaceful farm. Cut off by the hills. It was like a dream. Maggie ran round for hours, chasing hens, cleaning pigsties out, helping with the milking. For a long time she loved the life.

But then her mother took sick and she died seven months ago. Then there were just her three step-brothers, and the Big Man.

"My stepfather's part of the IRA," Maggie blurted out.

"You're kidding!"

"No I'm not. He's a Chief of Staff."

Tom, the old man, shook at that moment as if

35

someone had crossed his grave. Maybe he'd picked up the flu again, he was prone to that. He had to take better care of himself. Sometimes he didn't eat properly.

With that thought in mind he went looking for food.

Chapter Seven

"What does that mean?" said Karen.

"What? Being Chief of Staff? It means that he's the man in charge of the Provisionals. They go up to the north, around Newry, the bandit country. They organize ambushes and they bomb the security posts. I'm not supposed to know, but the whole village knows about it. It's safe there you see. We're like prisoners there."

"Is that why you left?"

Maggie started to think about it. *Was* that why she left? To escape from jail?

The brothers were angry and sick of life. They couldn't stand doing housework. And ever since Maggie had left that's all they *had* been doing. They were soldiers, they shouldn't be making beds.

"I'm well sick of this," said Declan.

"So tell me another," said Sean. "Why don't we just get a proper housekeeper? If she's not coming back – and she's been gone two weeks now – I'm not doing this for the rest of my life."

"The farm's bad enough," said William. "I've got the barns to clean. You've got it easy. I shouldn't do this."

"It's your flaming mess," said Declan.

"*I* didn't light the fire. I was the one who said the chimney's blocked."

"Like your head," muttered Sean as he threw himself down in a chair. "God, this place is a pigsty, it really stinks. I'm not cleaning that food up you know, I'll tell you that now, William. And you'd better clean it *fast*, 'cause there's flies on it. I'm not having maggots crawling all over the kitchen."

"You're a regular housewife!" William sneered at him.

"I'll put out your teeth for you!" Sean presented a warning fist. "I'm not looking after *you*, just 'cause you're a slob."

"Oh give it a break, will you?" Declan looked around wearily. "Da' will be coming home soon. Get this mess cleared up."

"Why – where are you going?"

"I'm going down the pub," said Declan.

"Ah – now that isn't fair!"

"We'll come with you!" said Sean.

38

Why did she leave? Her reasons were still confused, but mostly it was the lack of real freedom. The family wasn't cruel to her, the brothers might have teased her a bit, but they all liked her well enough, they were good to her. Her stepfather was kind, too, which was always a puzzle to her since he went around setting off Semtex bombs. It was just, being IRA, the family was under threat – from the police, from the security forces, from other terrorists. The biggest threat of all was from the real hard-line Protestants. The family lived in fear of the Protestants.

Maggie was only fourteen years old. She wasn't political and she didn't know what they were fighting about. Their own reasons seemed confused; when she eavesdropped from the top of the stairs, they were full of contradiction and murky truths. The one thing she was grateful for was that they never talked to her about it, they put no pressure on her to take part or clean their guns. They left Maggie out of it, though she knew what was going on. She'd have had to be blind if she *didn't* know. But they never spoke.

They went quiet when she walked in the room as if they'd already realized that this wasn't the kind of thing you talked about to a lonely girl struggling with growing up.

But most of the farm's visitors were hardly good company. Most of their visitors were terrorists.

And within this environment the family was virtually under siege. The farm became like a fortress. It kept them safe. It kept them safe from the violence, but numbed Maggie's life for her. She didn't want to spend her whole life as a cleaning girl.

And, also, she couldn't get over her mother's death. She missed her so much it was almost a physical pain. She couldn't remember her father dying, but her mother left an empty space, and it needed another woman to fill that hole. That's what she most needed, a woman she could call her own, for the life of the farm was the life of men. The only people she spoke to were Brady's three grown-up sons. She was protected from all else. She *suffocated*.

"Why did you run away, Karen?"

"Oh, you know, the usual stuff." Karen toyed with a blade of grass, twirling it through her hands and the sun shone from her hair as if it was made of gold. She sighed. "Nothing too much. I was mostly just bored I guess."

"But – no trouble?"

"No trouble. Just bored, Maggie."

Chapter Eight

The two boys were standing not far from Leicester
Square when a man came up and tried to sell them a
Walkman. He pulled it out of a bag and said, "The
genuine McCoy, brothers, look at all these features,
this thing can do just about anything. I mean, it'll
make you a cup of tea if you plug it in in the mornings
and *look at that*, it's even got anti-grav. Look at this
thing, brothers, I'm practically giving it to you. Look
at the size of it, you can fit that in a shirt pocket. I
mean *look at it*, feel the weight of it, do you see that,
it's got *no* weight. Do you know why? 'Cause it don't
run on batteries, boys. I'm telling you now, this is
state of the art, this is genuine solar-powered Walk-
manning. You go out in the sun, this'll blast both your
ears off. Just listen to that. No wait – got no tape in it.

41

Never mind that anyway, I'm practically giving it to you. Give me twenty-five quid, and this baby's yours. I mean, listen to that sound –" he shook the tape under Liam's ear. "You don't *get* better sound. This thing really hums."

"I couldn't hear anything," said Liam.

"'Cause it ain't got a tape in yet! You daft, kid, or what – I just said that! I'll sell you a tape look –" he reached in his jacket pocket. "No, I'll tell you what I'll do, I will *give* you a tape. Look at this here – what we got? 'Lectric Light Orchestra. Triffic tape that, you can have the lot. I'll throw in a box, too – you're practically robbing me. Don't come round again or you'll bankrupt me."

"We haven't got any money," said Liam.

"Why not? You wearing a watch?" said the man.

"No, we haven't got anything."

"Well get lost, kid. You're wasting my time. No, hang on just a minute there –" the man said as they turned to leave. "You want to earn a few bob selling Walkermans?"

"They just call them *Walkmans*," said Gerald.

"Not this lot, they're from Hong Kong. They don't work unless Jesus gets hold of them. But I'll tell you what I'll do, you're two smart kids, you can palm these off. I'll give you a fiver a throw, what d'you say, kiddo?"

Gerald looked uneasy. "I don't know," he murmured.

"Why not, you're already strapped for cash ain't you? Let's go for a drink, we can work out the details.

42

What d'you say, say we go and talk some business?"

The drink sounded good, and the two youths were ravenous, they hadn't eaten or drunk for a day or more.

"What about having some grub?" said Gerald.

"Oh sure, made of dough I am!" The man looked at them. "Oh come on, we'll get hamburgers."

He led them out of the main street into one of the side streets and hurried ahead as if they were already wasting time. He was wearing a long dirty coat, jeans with jagged tears in them, and his hair was tied back with a bow. Gerald noticed that he limped a lot.

"Are you coming or what?" said the man, as they hung back uncertainly.

They nodded. They needed the food too much.

After the park the two girls went to Trafalgar Square and sat for a long time just watching the traffic go past. They sat on the steps of the National Gallery while American tourists chattered by.

It was hot in the square. The sun hammered down from a sky that was virtually free of cloud. Traffic fumes hung in an almost palpable haze, and flocks of pigeons soared round on their flapping wings. All round the square people dodged through the growling cars, and every now and then somebody's horn sounded. It was like a huge ant colony with activity everywhere, and the black taxis prowled through like great fattened queens.

Karen said that at one time people cooled off inside the pools; but the pools were all empty now and the fountains were still. The lions had their tongues out as though they were panting, and only the statue of Nelson seemed to have found a breeze. Everyone else walked around sweating miserably, and trying to keep one step ahead of going raving mad.

After their trip to the park the two girls were now bored, and sat for a while without saying much. In order to remedy this Karen said that she'd throw up and teach it to Maggie to pass the time.

"I don't want to throw up," said Maggie.

"It's easy, I'll show you, look, you just push these two fingers down here like this –" Karen got to her feet and stuck half her hand in her mouth. "It's easy," she grunted, as her face became purple, and people around her started looking round warily.

A lady came up to Maggie. "Is that girl all right?" she said.

Maggie nodded. "She's trying to throw up," she said.

"What for? Is she ill?"

"No, I think she's just bored really."

"Oh." The lady walked off, but kept looking back.

"No, I can't get it up," said Karen, after gagging disgustingly for a while. "I think you're probably right, I'm just bored really."

Then she stood with her legs apart and her hands resting on her hips and she looked like the whole world belonged to her.

"It's a funny old world," she said thoughtfully. "I'm trying to puke me guts, and there's people pay a fortune for this rubbish." She jerked her head at the gallery. "A funny old world," she repeated.

Two seconds later she fainted.

The man took the two boys to the worst looking restaurant this side of a small town in Zambia. It was dripping with dirt, even flies tried avoiding it, and the light was so dim people strained their eyes. People could have gone blind in there and not noticed the difference, and the smell was something only a rat might know. Even rats might have had trouble putting their finger on it. It was a smell someone might have had amputated.

"What do you want, boys?" The man sat on a stool at the high, greasy counter and motioned a waiter to come across. It didn't matter too much because the waiter just turned his back. Even that wore him out. Simply breathing did.

They all settled for hamburgers and the long-haired man talked with his mouth full and kept spitting food on them.

"I'll tell you what I'll do," he said, as he gulped at a bottled Coke. "I've got five more recorders in the bag with me. I'll give them to you and I'll meet you here later on, and we'll see how you got on and talk some more. And don't do a runner 'cause I know what you look like. I'll find where you're living, I always do. 'Fact –" he crammed some more hamburger in. "It won't be worth doing it, 'cause I've got other lads do this sort of thing. You can make some good dough at it on a regular basis, so you play ball with me and you've got it made. What do you think, lads?" He watched their faces from across his plate, which he'd almost fallen into as he ate so fast. "Here, you just sit and have a look at them –" He handed a white bag to them, a bag that looked as if it had seen better days.

"It's good stuff, examine it. The genuine articles. Bankrupted stock, it's worth thirty quid."

"I think we can do it," said Gerald, taking a Walkman out. "And you give us five quid for all the ones we sell?"

"That's right," said the man, as he crammed the last of his food in his mouth and swilled it down with a long draught of tepid Coke. "You meet me at five and we'll see how you've done, okay?" Then he smiled a greasy, unpleasant smile.

Gerald nodded very sombrely, he thought he could manage this. But Liam wasn't too sure, and was feeling sick.

"You look hot – don't you want this?" The man took Liam's hamburger. "I'll see you later." He threw some money down and then he left.

The two boys sat a while then Gerald said, "Well, that wasn't bad."

"He just ate my hamburger!"

"It's a piece of cake really. We'll get twenty-five quid if we sell this lot."

"But he just ate my hamburger!"

"Oh do shut up moaning, Liam. Come on, let's go and make us some proper dough."

The old waiter watched them as they groped through near total darkness. He yawned – he was having a tiring day.

Selling Walkmans isn't as easy as it seems when you're having a hamburger. The boys stood in a street just off Piccadilly and Gerald tried just about everything to make a sale. He didn't have much luck, everyone just walked past him and most of them didn't even look at him.

"Excuse me –" he kept saying, but his words fell on deaf ears. There was no one who wanted to stop for the boys.

He took one of the Walkmans out of the carrier bag and said, "Right! I'm going to make sure they definitely stop!"

Liam didn't say anything. He was still feeling queasy. He had seen a cockroach on the restaurant floor.

"Excuse me –" Gerald stood in the way of two passers-by, two tourists with souvenir T-shirts on. The man was about thirty, with blond hair and tanned skin, and his wife was the same, only taller than him.

"Would you like a cassette player?"

"*Ja, Guten Tag. Wie geht's? Nein, wir sprechen kein Englisch. Wir sind Deutsch.*" The man gave a pleasant smile, and his wife was even more pleasant. They were so pleasant, they looked a bit barmy.

"Pardon?" said Gerald.

"*Nein, wir haben kein Geld. Wir sind auf Urlaub. Sind sie Englisch?*"

"Erm –" Gerald just stared at them. He licked his lips nervously. "Erm – would you like to buy one of these Walkmans?" he said. He stuck the cassette player under the German's nose. "Only twenty-five quid. It's the real McCoy."

"*Ja. Es ist sehr gut*," said the German, as he and his wife moved on. "*Wir haben ein zu Hause*,' he said, smiling back.

"What did he say?" said Gerald, turning to Liam.

Liam shrugged. "Something about going to the zoo," he said.

The old man was walking along the street, on the opposite side to the boys. He stopped to watch them; he remembered the pair of them from the incident back in the wine store.

He watched Gerald's attempts to palm off one of the Walkmans, which were growing increasingly desperate. And he watched Liam standing behind him, looking embarrassed, with his hands in his pockets and his expression glum.

They won't last long, he thought. They're a right pair of morons. And after a minute he carried on walking.

Chapter Nine

"So let me get this straight," said Karen. "You ran away from home, because you were like a prisoner on the farm in Dromiskin?" She had recovered from her fainting fit and was speaking very seriously, as though she was interviewing Maggie for a job she had. Her face wore a frown and her eyes crinkled as she talked. "But – so why did you come here, though, instead of just going to Dublin? I mean, what made you come down to London?"

They were still in Trafalgar Square, sitting on the gallery steps. It was still rush hour, and the traffic moved endlessly. They could hardly hear themselves speak and the sun beat down remorselessly. It was like sitting in the heart of a ship's engine.

Maggie considered the question and didn't answer

immediately. It was something she'd almost forgotten about. In the fear and excitement she'd almost overlooked her reasons. But now she was forced to confront them again.

It wasn't just the farm, that was only a part of it, it was mostly to look for her Aunty Jean. But why hadn't she done that? She had had Aunty Jean's address. How come she had ended up just roaming the streets at night?

She didn't speak for a while. She closed her eyes and let her thoughts drown out the sound of the growling cars. It was to do with uncertainty, and a new kind of fear she faced.

She was afraid Aunty Jean might not welcome her.

But why did she think that, when Aunty Jean liked her? She sent her birthday cards and sometimes sent letters to her. She hadn't seen her for a long time, except at the funeral, but she still somehow felt very close to her. But that feeling of closeness was when she was hundreds of miles away, and maybe Aunty Jean might feel differently face to face.

And she *had* run away and she still had a dad at home, even if he wasn't the dad who actually fathered her. Maybe Aunty Jean would feel funny about that. She might send her back again. Could she take Maggie in, with her own family?

Aunty Jean didn't like Maggie's stepfather too much, which might in the end make a difference. But which way would it go? Maggie didn't want to find herself turned away from the only door left to her. Now she'd finally arrived here, she'd filled up with doubt. And there was also the excitement, followed by the time that she'd spent alone and the fear which that brought, and the boredom. It was hard to get *motivated*. It was hard just to *do* anything. She had become stuck in a rut, and the feeling showed.

She knew that there was nothing to stop her looking up Aunty Jean's address in the phone book, but somehow she never got round to that. She kept putting it off a while. I'll just leave it a little while, I'll do it tomorrow, there's no real rush, she kept telling herself. Because she had it in reserve she could afford to postpone it a while. That's what she told herself, but mostly it was just the fear. The fear of rejection, the fear that she'd made a mistake, and the fear that she might not be loved enough.

Maybe losing the address was just part of the process, maybe she'd actually lost it deliberately. And though she knew the address was somewhere in Islington, she never tried wandering that way. She thought, maybe tomorrow, and put it off.

"Did you think no one would find you here?" Karen asked.

"I suppose so," Maggie mumbled, and Karen just nodded at this. She could understand that, she had felt much the same herself.

Maggie didn't say anything at all about Aunty Jean. She was Maggie's secret.

While she was thinking about this she suddenly became aware that a shadow had fallen across her and not moved away. She looked up to see two men in light-coloured business suits. They were smiling down happily at the two girls.

"Hello, ladies!" one of the men said. Karen glanced up and looked away. But Maggie wasn't sure quite where she ought to look.

The men were young and looked Middle Eastern, with deeply-tanned skin, brilliant teeth and almost identical hairstyles. Maggie thought they were brothers. They both wore gold chains round their wrists – *lots* of gold chains, like they made them. The first one kept smiling, but the other was more nervous. He kept glancing away, and then back again.

"We are here for our business," said the first. "And now it is finished. Very successful, we should both like to celebrate. Would you like to celebrate with us? We take you two for a drink. Would you like to have drinks? We could eat, too. What about sport? You ladies like sport? We could play tennis, we have joined in a sporting club."

Sport? Maggie thought. Play tennis in this heat? She looked at Karen, who was ignoring the men.

"Look," the first man said brightly, pulling his sleeve up. "You see this watch? A brand new watch, I just got it today. Look, it does everything – tells the time in Karachi, it tells you how deep you are – it does everything!"

"How deep do you think we are?" Maggie whispered to Karen, and the two girls started giggling. Then the men laughed too. The men didn't understand the joke but they laughed anyway. It was nice to be laughing. The men were happy.

"Would you like this watch?" the man said. "I give it to you, as a present." He started unclipping it. "Naman, give that lady your watch."

The other man jumped as if he'd been electrocuted, and started rapidly unfastening his own wristwatch.

Maggie was still uncertain how to react to this, but finally Karen turned round and looked at the men. "Save your watches," she said. "We're sitting here on our own, we don't want a drink, and we don't want to play stupid tennis. In fact, just leave us alone, will you? Mind your own business. Push off before we start screaming and call the cops."

"Yes?" The man was still smiling, as he didn't understand Karen. He didn't understand her accent or the way that she talked so fast. "You like to come play?" he said.

"I said *no*, go away!" said Karen. "We're covered in fleas, go away before they leap out all over you!" Then she started to laugh, and her arms gestured crazily. "*Mucho* fleas – understand? We've got fleas on us! *Si? You comprendez?*" The men looked bemused by her. Karen jumped up, laughing hysterically.

"Come on, Maggie," she said, dragging the other girl to her feet. "Tell them we don't even know where Karachi is!" And the girls ran off together, giggling delightedly.

The men stared after them, still smiling, waving their wristwatches.

Patrick Brady was making his way home to Dromiskin

53

from a 'business' meeting held in Ulster. He was driving his car through the lane that led up the hills. Grey sheep watched him, as their jaws chewed at clumps of grass.

Patrick Brady looked concerned, like he had a lot on his mind. He looked like a man who had lost something dear to him.

He pulled up as a group of sheep roamed round a corner, and the man who was shepherding tried to talk to him. But Brady didn't want to talk, and he wound the car window up. As the last sheep passed by, his car roared away.

The farmer stood watching him with his dog fretting at his feet. Then he shrugged, and ran after his wandering flock. It wasn't his business if Brady was in a mood. The dog raced on ahead to round up the sheep.

Two hours later the boys still hadn't sold a single Walkman and were growing disheartened.

"I thought you said it would be easy," said Liam, who was growing increasingly bitter. "If it's so easy, why's everyone ignoring us?"

"Because of your flaming face!" said Gerald. "Stop going on at me! If you can do any better, why don't you have a go? If you'd just try helping instead of standing there staring at everybody – you're like a zombie, no wonder they're scared to stop. If you're so full of ideas why don't *you* get us some money? At least I'm *trying*! All you're doing's moaning!"

Gerald jumped as a man suddenly appeared right

behind him and said, "What's that you got in the bag, boys?"

He was a stocky, well-built man, with a face like an ironing board, like he'd run head-first into a wall at some time. He had a lot of dark stubble and his eyes were like flecks of coal. He had a suit on, but the elbows were wearing through.

"I said what's in the bag, lads?" he said. "We haven't got all day you know. What you doing here – you got a licence for street-trading?"

"Er, no," said Gerald worriedly.

"We weren't doing anything," said Liam. "We were just standing here."

"Oh sure, trying to find out the time were you?" The man sneered unpleasantly. "Let's see in the bag, sonny." He jerked the bag out of Gerald's reach and looked inside. "Well, look at this here," he said. "Six brand new tape recorders. Which store did you nick these from, sonny-boy?"

It was generally Gerald who took the lead in things, but this time he was too frightened to say anything. It was left down to Liam, normally the timid one, to take a stand against all this rough treatment.

"We didn't steal them anywhere," he said. "A man gave them to us. And who are you anyway? We're not doing anything."

"Juvenile Crime Squad." The man hardly bothered listening to him, he was too busy going through the tape recorders. "We just had a tip-off about some kids flogging tape recorders." He closed the bag. "Do you want to tell me where you nicked them? Or do you collect the things?"

"A man gave them to us. I *said*," blurted Liam, who was rapidly losing his confidence. "We just met him this afternoon, he said we could sell them for him. He didn't say anything about licences."

"Where you boys from?"

"We're from Ireland."

"I don't mean that, I mean where are you staying?" The boys looked at each other.

"Just as I thought," said the man. "You're living out rough, are you? No fixed abode. You're in trouble, boys. You'll have to come down the nick while we check on these tape recorders. I assume we won't be *keeping you from anything*?" He said the last with a leer, and then seemed to dismiss them. He checked the street. "Where's John got to with that car?" he said. He took a deep breath and sighed and said, "You two wait here a minute, I'm going to bring round the car for you. Whatever you do, don't try to run away." Then with the bag under his arm he strode off looking for his car, and he turned round a corner and vanished from sight.

The two boys stood waiting, too afraid to try running away. They'd never been in any trouble with the police before. They didn't even try talking, they were too scared to say anything. They just stood there and waited, and bit their lips.

But ten minutes later they were still standing, waiting. Liam said, "I don't think he's coming back, Gerald."

"He's gone for the car," said Gerald.

"I don't think he has," said Liam. "I think he's just walked away with our tape recorders."

Gerald's expression turned to one of horror as realization suddenly dawned on him. "And you stood and let him?" he said furiously.

"Why, what were *you* doing?"

"I was waiting for *you*, Liam!"

Liam just sighed. He was past being surprised by now.

Chapter Ten

Patrick Brady called his eldest son, Declan, into the living room.

It was a quiet and peaceful room, the only sound was the ticking of a clock on the mantelpiece. There was a faint smell of woodsmoke and the scent of old furniture, the smell of leather, warm wood and hidden dust; the kind of smells you could find in a thousand old farmhouses, so familiar the men didn't notice it now.

Declan sat on the edge of an old leather sofa, and his father stood with his back to the room, looking from the window to the hills and the distant, grazing sheep. He hadn't yet taken his coat off; he'd come straight in from parking the car. His face was less worried, but had a sombre, more thoughtful look.

Beyond the window swallows were winging, but Patrick Brady did not really notice them. He didn't notice the sheep or the cattle in the lower fields. He didn't notice the hills, or the sea beyond. He had too much on his mind to be aware of these outside things. He had so much on his mind, he was all shut in.

Declan Brady sat quietly, aware that something was coming, and noticed that dust had built up on the ancient hearth. That was supposed to be Sean's job, keeping the fireplaces clean, but he'd neglected it, as they'd all started neglecting things.

Then his father turned slowly, as if it was an effort for him. He seemed older since Maggie had run away. He was a large man in his forties, a strong powerfully built man, but he seemed to have grown smaller, and hunched a little.

He ran his thick fingers through a mat of grey curling hair. His blue eyes, which were set wide in a broad, ruddy face, seemed to be looking at something that was miles away.

"Sit down there," he said, as though hardly aware of the fact that Declan had been sitting for some time now.

Declan, at 22, was the eldest of the three brothers. He shifted slightly on the sofa and said nothing.

"I think I've found out where she's gone to. I think that I've found where our Maggie's gone."

He took a pipe from a rack which stood on the mantelpiece, and didn't light it but stood quietly stroking it. Then he sat in the chair which stood closest to the fire, in his *own* chair, in the chair which he'd always had. It had seen better days; it was starting to fall apart and tufts of old horsehair poked out of it. But it was like an old friend, he felt safe when he used the chair. And he needed something to make him safe.

"I hoped, for a while," he sighed, "that she'd just gone to Dublin, but it looks like she's gone a lot further than that. We found that fool Gerald's motorcycle parked in the station yard. We asked around, and we think that she headed north."

"She went up to Belfast?" said Declan.

"Further than that," said Brady. "Some of the boys asked around the most likely spots. It seems that probably what happened, he must have come to the farm for her while we were away in the north on that 'business' trip. They went down on the motorcycle, hopped on the midday train, and went north, then by ferry to Liverpool."

"Maggie's in Liverpool?" said Declan.

"No, I don't think she is now," said his father. "I think that she carried on further than that. I think that I know where she's probably headed for, but I'll come on to that in a minute. That half-wit Liam Rourke's with them. What a crew those three make! A young girl, and two fools barely sixteen years. I know where they've gone to. There's nothing in Liverpool for them. They've gone to the bright lights. They've all gone to London, Declan."

Patrick Brady sighed heavily and stared in the fireplace. "Why in heaven didn't she just come and talk to me?"

Declan Brady said nothing. He didn't know what he ought to say because he'd felt much the same when he was Maggie's age. He hadn't run away from home but there were times when he'd wanted to. And he would have picked London. They always did.

"So what happens now?" he said, for the sake of saying something.

"I've got to go after her," said Brady.

"No! You can't go to England, Da!" Declan shouted; the thought was too horrifying.

Patrick Brady looked round. "She's my daughter, I have to go."

"But the Brits, Da!"

"I know about the Brits, Declan."

Patrick Brady sighed again and got up and paced round the room. "She's my daughter, I just have to *talk* to her, Declan. Try to find where we went wrong, what we did that was so wrong. See if maybe she'll want to come home again."

"But you can't go to England, Da!"

"It's the reasons I can't go that are the reasons that mean that I *must* go." Patrick Brady shook his head. "You can't keep this thing quiet, Declan, everyone in the town already knows about it. If word gets to the wrong ears there'll be people out looking for her. She's my daughter. I can't see her hurt, Declan."

"But – she's only your *step*daughter," said Declan out of sheer desperation. He was afraid of what his father was planning to do.

Patrick Brady turned angrily. "Don't you *ever* say

61

that again! She's my child, as much as you and the others are."

"But if the Brits get you, Da –"

"Or if the Brits get hold of *her*, Declan! Or the Protestants, or anyone – what am *I* to do?" Brady turned away angrily. "I can't turn my back on her, they'll hurt her in order to get at me. And there are things that they can't know, there's *knowledge*, there's *facts*, Declan, I can't let our enemies get hold of that. If they start to put pressure on me, well – I have to go after her. She's just a young girl – but they wouldn't care."

"Then I'll come as well," said Declan.

"No, stay here and guard the farm. I'll take one of the boys. Can't take too many."

"But how will you find her, Da?"

"We have plenty of friends over there. I can find her. I'll see if she'll come back home. Besides which I think that I know where she's gone to. I'll find her, or they'll have to kill me first."

His son Declan was silent. A gloom settled on the room.

"Our poor Maggie. She doesn't know what she's into," said Brady.

While Patrick Brady was making preparations to go to England to look for his daughter, a man in Dungannon was receiving a phone call which also concerned Patrick Brady's plans.

The man's name was Connor Cole, and he was

thirty-two years old. He was a calm, very quiet, very deadly man.

The voice said, "Ah, is that you? Is it you, Connor Cole?"

Cole said, "It is," in a voice which was so soft it seemed he didn't speak to the phone, but just breathed on it.

"Ah, good, I was hoping to catch you at this time. I was meaning to talk to you, Connor. We've got a small job, Connor, I was wondering how you might feel. Are you willing to travel to England, Connor?"

Connor Cole stood in silence. He was looking around his room. He'd worked hard to make his terraced home a comfortable place. "I'm not really interested," he said. "I've rather retired from that now."

"Sure that's just what I'd heard – but it's big, Connor."

"How big?" said Cole.

"You'll remember Patrick Brady, Connor? Well Brady's going to go over to England for a while."

"Brady's going to *England*?" Connor Cole's voice was raised slightly. "Sure he has to be mad, has he lost his mind?"

"It's over his daughter, Connor."

"Ah, yes." Connor Cole nodded. "I heard that his daughter's gone walkabout."

"Aye, she's run off to London. Young kids, Connor! What d'you do?"

"Aye." Connor Cole's breathing steadied. "They're a risk sure enough."

63

"Will you take on the job, Connor?"

"Just what has to be done?" said Cole.

"Well –" the other man became silent, as though he hadn't quite made his mind up on this, though in reality it was clear what he wanted done. "Well now, see – Brady's a danger, to us and to them, Connor, it would not be amiss to keep tabs on him. If it looks like he's going to prove some kind of danger, well, it might be as well to prevent that, Connor."

"And what if it doesn't look like Brady's a danger?" said Cole.

"Well – it might be as well he died anyway."

A long silence ensued while Connor Cole considered this, and his fingers toyed idly with a length of rope. Connor Cole had a sailing boat and was building another one. And sailing's not cheap, there are tools to buy.

"Aye, I could do," he murmured. "I could just keep an eye on him. How much is it worth?"

"Up to you, Connor."

Connor Cole nodded sombrely. "And then there's his daughter," he said. "What do I do if his daughter's there?"

"Well, we'll leave that to you," said the man. "You do what seems best, Connor. But we don't like loose ends. You just do what's best."

"Aye, I shall do," said Cole, and he replaced the phone carefully.

"I'll just do what seems best," he said to the room.

Chapter Eleven

While Patrick Brady was setting off for England, Maggie and Karen were wandering in Soho, in the mysterious streets of London's Chinatown. It was evening and the lights of the city were bright. It was warm, and the air had a heady scent.

Maggie couldn't remember ever feeling this good before. She delighted in her new-found friend's company. She felt strangely content, as though this life was for evermore, and she'd abandoned even looking for the missing boys. She never really thought that she'd find them again anyway, the chances of spotting them were slim. But it didn't really matter now, she had more faith in Karen's life. The two boys were idiots; she'd worked that out. If it wasn't for the boys she wouldn't have had all her money wasted on slot machines, video games and bits of junk. If it wasn't for the boys they could have got something sorted out, instead of just drifting like shadow-folk around the streets.

She didn't feel that she was drifting along now, she thought she had found something, a kind of friendship she'd never encountered before. Karen never wanted anything, she was content to take what she found. And Karen was considerably smarter than any boy. Unlike Gerald, she made no big deal about it. Karen just lived her life and didn't have to spin yarns about it. Karen took the blows and bounced back again.

But the boys would be moaning now – Maggie could picture them – they would probably be falling out and arguing. That's all they would do with their lives, they'd just moan about them. They would moan about all the things they thought that they lacked. They should have been like Karen, and just carried on with it.

The other thing that had happened was that she had almost forgotten her aunt, in the excitement of sharing in Karen's life. There was so much to think about and so many things to see that the thought had been pushed to the back of her mind. In a way this was deliberate; she was still holding on to it. It was the last dream she had; she was saving it.

Perhaps if she had known that things were soon going to alter, Maggie might have tried a bit harder to find her aunt. But at the time that was just a thought, there was too much to fill her mind. She didn't know that this time would soon come to an end.

She didn't know that this day, when she walked into Chinatown, was the last time she'd see her friend Karen again. If she'd known what was coming she would have dragged her friend out of there.

But then, Karen wouldn't listen. Karen never did.

"I'll tell you, Maggie, I'm absolutely starving. I could eat a horse, with its blanket for afters." Karen rubbed at her stomach which was grumbling alarmingly. "We're going to have to get something or I'll probably faint again." She looked down the street. "We'll try one of these supermarkets. "We'll have to get something or I'm gonna puke."

Maggie didn't demur at this. She never stole anything herself, but somehow it never seemed the same thing when Karen did it. "They're probably insured," she'd say. "And anyway we're starving to death. Nobody wants to see two little girls just *starve* to death." And then she'd quickly pick up something and put it inside her coat, and usually it was something they didn't need. Karen was not very selective, she'd grab the nearest loose object, whatever it happened to be. One time she came out with a complete set of saucepans, didn't know what to do with them, so returned and put them back again. Usually, though, she made a line for the food section. But what you were likely to wind up with was anyone's guess.

Today they had already eaten substantially; they had done some jobs at a hotel and were treated well.

But Karen was always hungry, she never stopped being hungry, it was a wonder she never put on any weight. Particularly with the food she ate, she was crazy for anything sweet. Maggie said that was why she kept fainting. If she ate a more balanced diet she'd probably feel better for it. Karen said, "Yeah, you're right, I'll start it tomorrow." But tomorrow never turned up in Karen's mind.

This evening her stomach was particularly ravenous, Maggie could hear it growling softly like a hungry dog. "We're going to have to really load up tonight, it's like I've got hollow legs. I haven't ever *been* so hungry. I must be sick or something."

Maggie said she would help by picking some stuff herself, but Karen wasn't happy with that idea. "No, you're too honest, Maggie, they'll see it all over your face. Just leave it to me, I know what I'm doing."

She led Maggie in to the first Chinese supermarket they saw, and groaned as she saw all the food laid out. It was only a small place – not like Sainsbury's – but they spent a long time walking round the aisles. The smell was intoxicating and the food seemed to scream at them, but it took a while to decide what they ought to take. A lot of labels were in Chinese and they couldn't make sense of them. Some of the food looked inedible, like chickens' feet.

There were ducks hung like toilet seats, flattened and gently smoked. There were live carp in fish tanks and bloated eels. Karen picked up a dried fish which looked like a table-tennis bat and said, "What do you do with this? Stick it on your feet?" She tossed it aside and picked a large box of crackers out. She tucked it inside her coat without looking round.

They passed a range of fresh fruit and Karen picked a few apples out. "I'll have to have some of these." They went inside her shirt.

Then she seemed to go crazy and started grabbing all kinds of stuff, until she was starting to waddle with the weight of it all. She looked like she was pregnant with all the food in her shirt, and she kept laughing and saying, "We'll have some of these!"

Maggie was nervous; they'd never taken this much stuff before, but so far no one seemed to have spotted them. Except for an old man who was following them carefully, a small grey Chinese man with staring eyes.

"Look at this, pickled eggs," said Karen, picking up a jar of small birds' eggs. "They don't even look real. Look like stones or something." She put the jar back on the shelf and at the same time picked up some cheese. At least she thought it was cheese; it was bean curd.

"Right, I think we've got enough," she said, which was something of an understatement, they could have fed anyone in the shop for a fortnight. And even as she said it the old man wandered up to them.

"I think you have something of mine," he said.

Karen looked at him for a moment. "Beat it, Maggie!" she said suddenly, and turned for the door and began to run.

The old man made a grab for her. Maggie said, "Leave her alone, you!" and she pushed him and he fell in a pile of cans.

"Come on, Maggie!" yelled Karen as she sped through the open door, and two young Chinese men set off in hot pursuit.

Maggie ran to the door. Everyone just ignored her now, all the attention was on the chase along Brewer Street. Karen ran like the wind, and her laughing voice drifted back. "Meet you later, Mags! Just got to lose these guys!" She was dropping food as she ran, but there was no time to pick it up. She kept running, and the young men were right behind.

They might not have caught up with her, she could run like a scared gazelle, but there was something ahead that the young girl had not yet seen. Maggie saw it though and began to run after her. "Karen! Don't go up there! There's a police car, Karen!"

Karen was laughing. She kept looking back at the men, and she still hadn't noticed the car ahead. It was parked right across the street and the driver was watching her. He said a word to his mate and they both climbed out.

Maggie stopped. It seemed everything found a terrible slow motion, and even the sounds of pursuit seemed to fade away. The old man had come out after her and was yelling something at the chasing men, and they called something back but Maggie didn't hear. It seemed all she could hear was the pounding of Karen's feet, and the sound of her own blood, beating like a drum.

She whispered, "Oh no, Karen," as the end seemed inevitable, and at the last second Karen, too, saw her fate.

She turned back with a desperate look. "Don't wait for me, Maggie! Beat it!" And the policemen grabbed both her arms.

"Run away, Maggie, *run*!"

And Maggie did; she just turned away and ran. There was nothing else that she could do.

She ran away, and had to leave her best friend behind.

Chapter Twelve

London was a lonely place for Maggie now. For the next twenty-four hours she wandered around in a daze, visiting the places that Karen usually frequented but finding no sign of her missing friend. She was probably arrested; perhaps she had been sent back to Sunderland. Maggie didn't know what had happened, but she knew Karen had gone. She could feel it like a change in the air, like a cold breeze that blew through her. Like a doorbell which rings in an empty house.

But still she kept wandering, hoping to find Karen. Until as night fell she knew it was time to stop. She wouldn't find her now, there were a million places she might sleep. Maggie had to find her own sleeping place. She'd been taught that much.

She hadn't eaten for several hours but still couldn't

find her appetite, even though there was a constant kind of grumbling inside her stomach. She knew that really she had to eat, it was what she kept telling Karen to do, and in Charing Cross she got lucky and found a coin. It was only a pound but it would get her some supper for the night. She went into a snack bar and settled down.

That was one thing she'd learned, that you made all your meals drawn out. If you ate food too quickly you wanted more. So she ordered a Coke and a small dried-up sponge cake and took them both to a corner seat and huddled down. She kept low like Karen told her to, so you didn't attract attention. She wrapped her hands round the can of Coke, and sipped at it.

It was a cheap place, the lighting was poor and the furniture had clearly seen better days. The tables were greasy and the chairs were all rickety, but Maggie didn't notice that; she was too tired to care. All she wanted to do was to sleep and forget about things. But it gets hard to sleep when you're on your own.

Two boys were playing noisily on an old video game machine and they kept glancing her way, but she didn't look. They were trying to show off for her, but they were whistling against the wind. Maggie was beyond being impressed by two stupid boys. She felt old now, much older than when she first came from Ireland. She felt that the city had made her mature quickly. Living rough usually did that to you, you had to survive. But you grew up too fast, you left childish dreams behind.

The owner was watching her. He was a kind man with a child of his own, a daughter who was about Maggie's age. He could see that something was bothering her and that the two boys planned to talk to her. She didn't need that, it was obvious.

He poured out a big mug of tea and ambled across to her. On the way he picked up a small plate of cakes. He was a short, rather fat man with a round face and balding head. He looked like he might have been Greek, but he was London-born.

As he sat in the seat opposite her and scowled at the two boys to make them leave, he saw that Maggie had two teardrops rolling down her cheeks. She hadn't even noticed him, she was miles away, lost in thought. He smiled at her. "Is it really that bad, little lady?"

Maggie looked up with a frightened, surprised expression. "I'm sorry," she said, and got ready to leave.

"No finish your drink," he said, gesturing her back again. "I'm not telling you to leave. I brought cake with me, look."

He looked round the snack bar which was practically empty now. The two boys were hanging round, not prepared to leave. "I'll be closing up soon," he said. "Not too much trade now I think. And I'm getting too tired. I'm just getting old."

He slid the mug of tea towards her and said, "Why don't you have this, too. It'll help warm you up, it gets cold at night."

"I haven't got any money –" she said.

But the man waved her fears away. "Have some cake, too, they'll only go off tonight. I was going to throw them out anyway, put a few in your bag, look. Here, I've got a paper bag, put some cake in here."

"Thank you." Maggie smiled at him.

"You don't look a happy girl."

"I lost someone," Maggie said. "I lost my friend."

"Ah." The man nodded slowly. "That's sad, we all need a friend. Don't you have any other friends, or a family somewhere?"

"No." Maggie said this too quickly to avoid being lectured by him. She had the feeling all grown-ups were lecturers.

"Ah." He shook his head sympathetically. He seemed to believe her, which is really what matters most. If he had any doubts he kept them to himself.

He scratched at his head as he stared at the table top, and flicked off some grains of sugar which had spilled across. "It's none of my business," he said, "but you should think about going home. It doesn't get any easier. I've seen it happen."

"Go back to Ireland?" said Maggie.

"If that's where you're from," he said.

"I can't."

The man shrugged. "Well, just think about it. Where will you stay tonight?"

"I'll find somewhere," Maggie said.

"Have some more cake," he offered, pushing the plate at her. "You know, tomorrow you might not be as lucky as this, you might not get anything at all to eat. What are you going to do then? Will you live off the fresh air? Will your dreams be enough to keep hunger away?"

"I don't eat a lot," she said.

"No, but we all need *some* food in us. Just think about it will you, about going home? It's easy to forget, you get caught in this sorry life. Do you remember what it is that you're looking for?"

Maggie thought hard with a frown which the man was familiar with from his own daughter struggling with growing up. "I thought – I maybe did once," she said. "But it all got mixed up a bit and –" she tailed off, the words simply dried up on her.

"It's not what I thought it would be," she said. "And now my friend's gone away."

"It's no fun growing up," he said.

"No, it's not."

"Listen," he said, then he turned round and saw the two boys staring at them, they'd both become suddenly silent. For some reason they annoyed him, they were typical of all the boys who came in here to spend their time playing the slot machines. They never bought any food for themselves but pushed a fortune into the slots. He didn't know where they got it from, but they lost it all. They were so bored that often they managed to irritate him.

"What are *you* looking at?" he said angrily. "Go on, just clear out of here. We're closing." He got up and shooed them away. "You've got more money than sense anyway, go home to your own homes!" And he slammed the door and then slid the sign across.

"Stupid dumb kids," he said, as he sat down at Maggie's table. "Waste all of their money on slot machines. What were we talking about?"

Maggie shrugged, she could barely remember. It seemed they weren't talking of anything.

"Look," the man said, "I know it's none of my business, but where were you planning on staying tonight?"

"I don't know," said Maggie, and shrugged her slim shoulders again. "I don't know. I'll probably find somewhere."

"Just what I thought," he said. "You'll be sleeping out rough again. That's dangerous, look, here –" and he reached in his pocket. He took a few notes out and slid two across to her. "Try to find somewhere decent to stay tonight. And maybe tomorrow – well, think about going home. If it's bad, it can't be much worse than this you know."

Maggie looked at the money, her eyes almost mesmerized. "I can't just take your money," she whispered.

The man seemed to dismiss it. "It's nothing, small change," he said. "But do me a favour, get yourself something good with it. Get yourself a bed, get some food –"

"Yes, I will," she said.

"And if you're hungry tomorrow, come back again. I can give you some food but – it won't last forever. There's no future in walking the streets you know."

Maggie nodded. "I know," she said, and the man

almost wept for her; he could imagine his own daughter in this position. And this girl was so gentle, he could see it just by her face. She wasn't tough enough. Very few kids were tough enough.

"Well, okay," he said awkwardly, not knowing what more to say. "I've got to lock up now, you'd better be on your way."

"Okay." Maggie stood up, and picked up her Coke and cakes. "You're – thank you very much," she said.

"You're welcome, kid." It's nothing, he thought. It's a drop in the ocean. And he sighed as he watched her walk out the door.

And a few minutes later as he was clearing the snack bar up, he saw that she'd left her small rucksack beneath the table.

He waited a while, but she did not come back for it. He sighed again as he stowed it behind the door.

But while Maggie at least had some food and some money to spend, the two boys were becoming increasingly desperate.

They had lost all their money, their belongings had been left behind, and now the man with the tape recorders would be after them. It wouldn't matter to him if they said they'd been stolen, even if he believed them he'd still want his money back. Their whole dream had turned sour on them and Liam was worn out with it. Liam thought it was time to go home again.

But Gerald was stubborn. He wanted to carry on. Gerald was an absolute fool as far as Liam was concerned.

If he could only get rid of Gerald and walk into some police station. He was sure they'd look after him. They would send him home.

Or would they? There were so many roaming the streets these days, would they really be interested in Liam Rourke? Gerald said they would lock him up for being a vagrant. And Liam was scared that for once his friend could be right.

So he followed Gerald aimlessly, hoping against hope that something would turn up and get them both out of this. But he didn't think it would when they turned round a corner and a nightmarish sight met into his eyes.

"What's this?" he said horrified, as his feet were rooted to the spot.

"This is where we're going to have to bed down for a while."

"We can't stay round here," said Liam.

"Well, where else do you want to go? We haven't got too much choice, Liam. We've run out of ideas, this is all that's left."

But Liam still couldn't make himself take a step forward. "Not in this place," he whispered. "Don't make me stay here, Gerald."

"We have to. Cardboard City is the only place left for us."

Chapter Thirteen

The next morning Patrick Brady arrived in England aboard a fishing boat which docked in a Cornish port. He slipped away quietly with a bodyguard to watch his back, and went straight to the station and booked a train. They arrived in London in the late afternoon and went straight away to one of their safe houses. The IRA has quite a few of them dotted around, in much the same way as they find people everywhere who support them with funds for 'the cause'.

Patrick Brady had the feeling that he knew where his daughter had gone, and he would check that this evening after having some rest. It had been a rough crossing and he wasn't a good traveller, but he couldn't travel in the way that the public could. He needed just to get his head down for a while and then make some enquiries. He wanted to stay for the shortest time possible. There were too many prying eyes and too many blabbing mouths. It wasn't safe to be over here. It was quite a risk.

He would ask round his contacts, and he had quite a few of them; the IRA seems to find support everywhere. And the Irish stick together, as most people do in foreign parts. He was sure he would find her; it was just the time. The longer he stayed here, the greater the risk became. He was nervous; it was not like his fortress home. This was enemy territory, his foes would be everywhere. He hoped they hadn't got to his daughter ahead of him.

The thought made him nervous as he settled to get some sleep. "Watch the door, Ryan," he said, as he closed his eyes.

Ryan nodded. He would, he was loyal to Mister Brady, though he had a few doubts about this enterprise. He would have had even more doubts if he'd known who was waiting for them in a hotel a few miles from where they stayed.

For Connor Cole was ahead of them, already getting prepared for them. Wiping dust from a handgun, and thinking hard.

Chapter Fourteen

The next afternoon Maggie returned to the snack bar to look for her bag.

It was busy now; there were people sitting at her table and the owner was rushing about frantically. But he spotted Maggie standing by the door and immediately stopped what he was doing.

"You take over," he told the young girl who helped him, and she scowled at him because she was already rushed off her feet.

"I've got your bag here," he said, as Maggie hung in the doorway, reluctant to enter the busy place. "I thought you weren't coming back for it."

"I'm sorry, I forgot," she said.

"Did you get somewhere to sleep?"

"Yes, I did," she said.

"Good, what about some food?" he said. "Are you feeling hungry?"

"No, I've had something," said Maggie. "Thanks anyway." Maggie was lying, she hadn't had anything yet, but it didn't seem right taking too much from this man. She knew he was kind and was genuinely concerned for her, but all the same, she had to stand on her own two feet.

"Right." The man seemed to become a little awkward then; he didn't know what else to say to her. And his customers were clamouring; they all wanted feeding.

"Well, I'll just get your bag," he said finally. As he ducked below the counter to pick up the bag he stuffed a few bread rolls inside it. Then he glanced about furtively to make sure no one was looking, sneaked some cash from the till and shoved that in too.

"Here you are," he said, standing up and handing the bag back to her. "If you get hungry then call again later. But don't make a habit of it!" He was trying to make a joke of it, but they both knew they'd gone as far as they could go. Maggie wouldn't be coming back again, and he'd done his best for her; that was as much as was needed.

"Right then – good luck," he said, and he held out his hand to her.

Maggie shook it. "You're a very kind man," she said.

"Yeah, well – you just take care," he said, a little embarrassed now. "You're a very nice kid." And they smiled at each other.

Then Maggie walked away and his overworked girl said, "What was all that about there then?"

"Oh, go back to your work!" he said, suddenly irked at her.

"Ooh, suit yourself!" she said tartly. "I'm only asking!" Then the girl sulked for the rest of the day and they didn't talk again until closing time.

But the man didn't care, the daft girl probably deserved to sulk. It was Maggie he was worried about. Her cares were real.

After leaving the snack bar Maggie walked through the streets for a while, half-heartedly looking for Karen. She knew she wasn't going to find her but could find nothing else to do. She was becoming morose. It was bound to happen.

After a long time spent sitting on a bench in a quiet park, she did something she hadn't done for quite a while. She went into a church, just to enter its solitude, and feel its peace around her. Just to say a prayer.

The air inside was cool. Sunlight entered through a high, stained-glass window and fell on the floor in small pools of colour. It looked like a rainbow that had fallen to pieces, and there was no way to put them back together again.

Maggie lowered her bag. There was nobody in the place, and no sound but the traffic noise filtering through. She walked up the long centre aisle and made a sign to the golden cross, then she sat on a pew, and bent her head in prayer.

She kept her head down for a long time, although she'd run out of things to say. She wasn't sure what she *should* say, but it didn't matter. God would already know all the things she'd been going through. If He cared He would help her. He would read her thoughts.

And anyway Maggie wasn't sure if she wanted God to help her, it seemed like a cheek to fall back on Him. He had other things to do, a lot more things than she could ever count. He had *big* things to care for, not little girls.

She was still praying quietly a considerable time later when a priest appeared from a door at one side of the church. He was only half-garbed and his collar was hanging loose. He wasn't expecting to see anyone, he was in a hurry.

He didn't seem to notice Maggie as he went about his duties, pausing to bow his head each time he passed the altar, and crossing himself almost unconsciously. He was young and his hair was long. He hurried because the Father would be coming soon. He would be coming back to check that he'd got the place tidied up. He had slept in too long, and now he had to rush.

He paused as he saw Maggie who was still bent over her prayers. Should he talk to her? Perhaps not, he had things to do. And the girl hadn't noticed him, though she must have heard him rushing about. If she needed him she would speak to him; he carried on.

But a few minutes later he almost jumped as

Maggie appeared almost silently behind him. "Can I make a confession, Father?"

"I'm afraid I'm not the priest," he said. "I'm only a novitiate. And this isn't the time for Confession – can you come back on Thursday?"

"Oh. No, it's all right." Maggie turned away wearily.

He frowned as he watched her go back to her seat and look round for her bag, which was by the door. She was getting confused; she was starting to misplace the bag. This was the second time already that she'd lost the thing.

"No, hang on a minute," he said, as he watched her fumble under the pew. "If you want to see the Father, I'm sure he'll make time for you."

"No, it's okay," she murmured. "It doesn't really matter now." She seemed baffled. She seemed almost half-asleep.

"Your bag's by the door," he said softly. "But won't you sit down for a while? It would give me a break just to talk a while."

Maggie shrugged. "If you like," she said.

The young priest smiled. "I've got nothing else to do, I've only got to count up the books now."

He sat down beside her and simply stared ahead for a while, looking at the altar and waiting for the girl to speak. But she was embarrassed to speak, for priests were important men. They were the next thing to God, and you didn't waste their time. And maybe she was wasting his time if she talked of her own troubles. Maybe she ought to leave. But she was *so* tired . . .

"Father," she whispered, gathering her courage up, "would it be a sin if you ran away from home because you were unhappy?"

The young priest considered this. He wasn't a Father, he wasn't trained to deal with people's confessions yet. But he was a young man, and he knew what it's like to be troubled. He said, "The family's important. It's the home of God."

"I thought this was His home?" she said.

"But God resides everywhere. In the family is where He's most welcome."

"Oh." Maggie was silent, this wasn't what she had hoped to hear; she was getting mysticism when she wanted some practical advice. "Do you think I should go home then?"

"What do *you* want to do?" he said.

She didn't know, but her home did seem tempting now. She was thinking of it more and more, of its warmth and its pleasant smells, of the wind in the rafters and the lazy cat.

But if she went home, would her life be the same again? Could she put up with that? Could she go back to it? Aunty Jean didn't seem so good, she already had her own family. Was she just an excuse, and a chance to get away? She was even missing her father. She'd stopped calling him "stepfather". He *was* her own father. He cared for her. If she went back and talked to him, maybe he'd understand. They never did talk much, and that was wrong. It was wrong to keep things all bottled up.

"What's your name?" she heard the priest saying.

"Maggie."

"Mine's John."

"Oh." She was silent again. She didn't know what to say to him, there were too many thoughts tumbling round in her mind. Sitting quietly had given her the chance to think.

"Could I be on my own?" she said rather embarrassed.

"Yes, of course." The man nodded, and went away.

She sat for a while thinking of her own father, and their Father in Heaven, then she rose to leave.

Chapter Fifteen

After his good luck a few days before, the old man was going through a sticky time. But this was how it went sometimes, it was an up and down life, living on the streets, with no guarantees and no promises. Sometimes you'd get to a place and they had plenty of jobs going – hotels and restaurants often wanted staff. Nothing too permanent, just a couple of hours cleaning up, enough to pay for your lunch or a loaf of bread. Other times you got there and they didn't need anyone, or someone had beaten you to it. It was all down to luck. There was no use complaining about it. Complaining never got people anywhere.

But that was how it had been lately, other people beating him to the jobs, to the handouts, to the soup-wagons – he was always too late.

He was getting depressed about it. He was also starting to get hungry, and he wasn't having any luck with his begging. There were so many beggars around these days, people didn't bother stopping any more – they were too used to it, it was just one more street-hazard. And a lot of them these days weren't even real beggars, they were professionals, they were making a living at it. The old man had no time at all for them.

The old man was grumpy. If he thought about it properly he probably wasn't depressed, he was just moody because his run of luck had taken a downward turn. That was the trouble, you started getting used to it, you thought that maybe you *were* lucky, and that was a mistake. You couldn't take anything for granted, least of all lucky spells, you just got greedy, and then you got knocked down again. It was only life's balance keeping everything in perspective. That's why they called the thing pot-luck. It was only fair.

Except *some* people seemed to be having a lot better luck than *he* was having. And that made him grumpy. It made him mean.

He was walking around Piccadilly hoping to scrounge something, but he was in too much of a bad mood for that to work. People weren't over-friendly when you were walking around breathing fumes, they wanted *nice* people, and a nice class of street-vagrant. "Ah well, suit yourself then," he kept muttering as he grumbled all along the street. "I hope I starve to death, and then you'll feel sorry for me."

He stopped. He had seen something which made his eyes start to bulge. His heart hammered in his chest. His breathing stilled.

Just a few yards ahead there was a woman with an open bag, and on the top of the bag was a leather pouch. The pouch was bulging with money! He could hardly believe his eyes. There were *thousands* of pounds! They had to be Yanks, he thought.

He looked up. Yes they were, they were two loud-mouthed Texan folk, a fat man with an even fatter wife. They had gaudy check shirts on and white baggy trousers. They looked morons, but they were dripping with Yankee cash.

The old man didn't often steal money, he had certain principles, but he was starving, and those berks deserved their luck. Walking around town like they practically owned the place; they probably *did* own half of Texas, they'd never know. She'd probably say, "Oh look, Clyde, I dropped it!" and they'd go to the nearest American Express office and load up again and get that nicked, too.

But could he do it? Could he bring himself to steal in broad daylight? Maybe it was wrong, he'd only get into trouble for it. You take stuff like that then no good's bound to come of it. So he opted for a more honest line of work.

He licked his lips nervously and walked up behind the man. "Excuse me, sir – could you spare me a bob or two?"

The man turned around. "Hey get lost, buddy! Take a hike!" Old Tom stared in amazement. You stingy git! he thought.

Right then, that did it, he was definitely going to steal it now, that bill-fold was as good as in his pocket! He waited till they turned away then licked his twitching fingertips. You've had it now, Buster. That purse is mine!

But Tom never got that far. Before he could make a move a young guy ran past and whipped out the leather pouch.

"Oi!" Old Tom couldn't believe it. "Oi, come back, that's my money!" he said. And he started to run after him, punching the air.

The American couple looked amazed, then the woman said, "That's my money, Duke!" And old Duke started lumbering in hot pursuit.

"You come back here, you little git!" Old Tom's mind was working overtime. If he rescued the money, he'd be a hero; they were bound to reward him then. He could see it already, he could feel it in his fingers – they would make him rich.

He just had to catch the bloke, who was running like a whippet now, with old Tom far behind like a lumbering horse. "*Ha!*" He saw the boy start to slow, he must have picked up a stitch or something. "I'll get you now, kid!" Tom was going wild. If he could just get his hands on the kid and wrestle him to the ground he might pick up some injuries and *then* they'd care.

They might put him in hospital, he could see it all now, being looked after by nurses who knew what a star he'd been. They'd really take care of him, there'd be Lucozade and purple grapes, there'd be clean sheets and hot baths and stodgy food. If he could only get hold of the kid, if he could just gain another yard, and then – "*Oof*!" he said as somebody clobbered him right in the back. Old Tom pitched forward, groaning.

"I've got you now, you dumb sneak-Limey purse-snatcher!"

Old Tom looked up as big Duke towered over him.

"It wasn't me, you great berk, it was him!" he said. He rubbed at his shoulder. "It was me trying to help you! You stupid great Yankee banana!"

"Who?" said the American, peering down the street.

"The young kid with the glasses on! He's gone now!"

The American peered at him. "Gee, I'm real sorry, bud." Then he turned on his heels and just walked away.

"Hoi! What about me?" said Tom.

"I can't help you now, buddy. We just lost all our dough, that's the way it goes."

The old man couldn't believe it, he just sat in the street and thought this was really not one of his better days. And then he looked up, and it was starting to rain on him. He sighed. He should have stayed in bed today.

He overheard somebody walking past say, "So where is it then, this Cardboard City?"

"It's only a place," said another voice.

"But what kind of place is it?"

"It's some crazy place where the down-and-out weirdos go."

At least that's not me, thought Tom. I ain't ever sunk to that level. He hoped he was never going to have to.

Cardboard City: a place of shadows and whispers and flickering fires; a place where the night can be filled with the sound of sighs.

For two days the boys hung on the fringe of this murky place, and on the third night they penetrated deeper. It was strangely quiet and strangely dark, with a darkness compounded by flickering fires. Slow figures moved like grey ghosts or the shades of men. From the hollows dark eyes looked out, watching them.

The boys walked slowly, barely breathing, keeping close to the road's edge and a chance of flight. They didn't want to go too deep but they seemed to be beckoned on, by the light of the fires and the whispering night. They were scared and their fear showed in the way they hung close together, and the way they hunched down, like the night was cold.

All along the way people were settling down for the night – old people, young people, men and women. They were sorting their boxes out, so packed they could hardly move; they were checking the wind flow to thwart the draughts. There were so many boxes, of all shapes and sizes, it was hard to know where the people found them all. And every box had its owner, there was no waste at all around; if something looked to be spare, someone pounced on it. They were always on the look out for some extra warmth, for one more scrap of paper to plug the gaps. Some were quite tidy, and others just clumsy heaps. But each space had its owner, and each box was home.

By this time a lot of people were settling down for the night, becoming invisible, shielded by cardboard walls. Others were huddled around crackling fires, tossing on anything that their cold hands could find to burn. There was laughter and murmuring and occasional argument. There were scuffles over borders and boundaries. Every now and then someone's voice lifted in anger. There was the sound of glass smashing, curses and drunken cries.

But most people were quiet. It was almost unnaturally quiet, as if all these people just hid away. They didn't want to draw attention to themselves; they didn't want any trouble. They had built up this city to protect themselves.

For two days the two boys hung on the edge of this nightmare land. But now they were desperate. And they tried to join.

"What do you think we do?" whispered Liam. "Do we just take some boxes or what?"

"I don't think so, they've all got someone in them," said Gerald.

"So what do we do?" said Liam. "There's no space left anywhere, it's all chock-a-block. Do we just squeeze in?"

"I don't know," muttered Gerald.

"Do you think we should ask someone? What do you think, Gerald?"

"I don't *know!*" Gerald said. He was feeling tense. "I'm trying to think, will you give me a break for a while?"

"I'm going to ask this man here," Liam said suddenly. It seemed weeks since he'd last had a decent night's sleep, and now he was desperate to get some rest. "Excuse me –" he said, but the man turned away from him.

"Just forget it," said Gerald. "We'll find somewhere." He looked down the street which had taken an eerie hue as more and more fires started springing up. There were shadows thrown everywhere, like a ballroom of dancing ghosts. A thick smell of smoke wafted over the boys.

"The first thing to do," said Gerald, "is to find a few boxes somewhere. We'll have to go back to town and see what we can find."

"But where will we go?" said Liam. "There's no space left anywhere. Look, they're right in the road. We'll get killed, Gerald."

"We're not going to get killed!" said Gerald, who was taking a firmer role. "We'll just look around, we're bound to find something." He was feeling a lot stronger now that he'd found a direction. They had somewhere to go. He had toughened up.

"We'll be all right, Liam. Just trust me, we'll be all right."

Liam wanted to trust him. But he was scared to death.

Chapter Sixteen

They weren't the only youngsters to be having problems. In another part of town Alan Foster was also about to encounter a problem, although he didn't know it yet.

Alan Foster was sixteen years old and something of a paradox in that he looked a lot older yet sounded considerably younger. He wasn't a bright kid; people said he was dim, mentally retarded. But he wasn't retarded, he was just a bit slow. There's no crime in taking your time over things.

He had a round chubby face and curly blond hair, and he flushed a lot when he was nervous. When he was nervous he was inclined to get flustered and he'd shout a lot and wave both his arms about. Because his friends found this comical they had a tendency to wind him up just in order to *see* him get flustered. But this wasn't Alan's fault, it was really his friends' doing. Alan could have done with a few better friends around.

He lived with his mother and his two elder brothers in a Council flat on the south side of Islington. His brothers were hooligans; they were in trouble with the law all the time. They were criminals, at the small end of the market.

But Alan looked up to his brothers, not because they were criminals, but because there wasn't anybody else to look up to. And he was impressed by the things his brothers used to tell him, although most of it was total invention. His brothers used to brag a lot about the things they'd been up to, and Alan believed every word of it.

In truth, his brothers did have some notoriety because they *were* villains, if only very small ones. The kind of things they went in for were housebreaking and petty theft, and occasionally 'leaning on' shopkeepers to get them to pay for protection so their shops weren't smashed up. Mostly it was relatively minor crime, but they were probably headed for bigger stuff.

Alan himself didn't participate in their crimes because his brothers didn't think he was smart enough. They didn't even tell him about most of their *real* crime, because they didn't trust him to be able to keep his mouth shut. They kept making promises about how they'd take him along one day, but it was just a kind of gentle fun poked at him. In a strange kind of way his two brothers looked after Alan, because they recognized that he wasn't too smart at life. They tried to steer him away from trouble because he was certain to get it wrong. He would wind up in trouble while the rest escaped. He just wasn't bright or *quick* enough. He'd still be standing there while everyone else ran away.

Unfortunately Alan's brothers weren't there when he needed them. When one of the Boote twins called round, only Alan was in. Joey, his eldest brother, was in the local remand centre, and Billy was staying at his girlfriend's place.

The one thing they'd warned him about was to steer clear of the Boote brothers. "They're head-cases, they'll get you into trouble, Al."

Alan was scared of the Bootes but had a certain respect for them. They were *real* villains; they'd already made it big. They were still only young but they'd already been "inside". They had robbed building societies. They were Big.

They also had tattoos, which impressed Alan.

"Hello, Al, your brother in?" Stevie Boote lounged across the step.

"Which one?" said Alan nervously.

"Your Billy."

"No," Alan said. "They're both out. There's no one in."

"Oh. That's too bad," said Stevie. He stopped to think. When he was thinking he had the habit of staring at his shoes. Then he looked up suddenly. "Are you doing anything, Al?"

"Um – doing what?" said Alan, who was already getting flustered. Being around Stevie was enough to make his stomach quake. "I'm having my tea," he said.

"No, I mean in the morning. We need a lookout, do you fancy a job, Al?"

"Who, me?" said Alan momentarily taken aback by the offer. He couldn't believe it – they were asking *him* along? "Erm, I don't know," he said. "I don't think so."

"Good." Stevie nodded. "We'll meet you in the morning outside Hanratty's fish shop, about ten. Do you know the place, Al?"

"Er – yeah." Alan jerked his head.

"Good." Stevie grinned at him with a dark, greasy, furtive look. "We'll see you in the morning then. Keep it under your hat, Al."

"Yeah." Alan nodded again as Stevie seemed to just fade away, melting in the evening like a breath of fog.

Alan closed the door quietly and stood for a time thinking about this. Then he went in the kitchen and made some tea.

This was a turn up for the books, the Boote brothers asking *him* along. They were part of the big league. This would really impress his brothers when he told them, he could really show what he was worth then. Alan had always believed he had something to offer, if he could only find a way of expressing it. And this was the break he'd been hoping for. He'd always looked like a big kid, now he could prove he was. This would stop them all laughing when they heard about it. Alan Foster and the Boote brothers. Boy that was something. They'd really start taking him seriously then.

He became almost hyperactive as he rushed round the tiny flat, bursting with a secret that nobody else knew. Even his own brothers were scared of the Boote brothers. And he would be actually *working* with them!

In all this excitement he forgot all the warnings. As he had forgotten to ask just what his role entailed.

It was only much later when he was lying in his room alone that he thought, I wonder what I *am* doing in the morning?

Chapter Seventeen

Trying to stay in Cardboard City had not been a good experience for the boys. They'd kind of hoped that with them being in much the same boat as everyone else, they would be willing to help each other. But it didn't work out like that; everyone had a jealous streak, everyone wanted to hold on to the things they had.

The boys had found a few boxes at the back of an electrical store, and gone back with them and tried to bed down for the night. But, like Liam said, there was no room left anywhere, they had to try squeezing in, which was a big mistake.

Maybe they were unlucky in the places they tried to fit, but all around them angry voices kept moving them on.

"You can't sleep round here, kid! There's no room here, bugger off! You turned up too late, you've got to stake your claim."

And somebody else said, "If you put that box there, laddy, I'm gonna come over there and let you know all about it!"

They tried bedding down on the edge of the pavement, but that didn't work either because they ended up blocking the footpath. A policeman moved them on. "You can't cause an obstruction, lads. You'll have to move somewhere else, you can't settle there."

"But there isn't anywhere else!" said Gerald.

The policeman shrugged. "That's too bad," he said. "You can't bed down there. Go on, move along." And he watched as they wandered off until he was sure that they'd cleared the street, and then he went back to his normal patrolling.

There aren't any favours given to you if you're homeless; no one's paid to look after you. You are out on your own; the boys were learning that.

They nearly got into a couple of fist-fights with other youths who were after their boxes. In the end they just gave their boxes away, they weren't tough enough to resist the attacks. They ended up where they started, three days ago.

Liam was desperate, he'd just about given up by now. He said, "Maybe we ought to go home, Gerald."

"What, go back to Ireland?" said Gerald.

"Yeah." Liam squinted. "What do you think about it?"

103

"We can't go back until we've got Maggie with us."

"But they'll understand," said Liam, "it wasn't *our* fault, Gerald. I mean, it's easy to lose someone *here*. The police will start looking for her, we're not going to find her. Let *them* look, they know what they're doing."

Gerald was frowning, it wasn't even worth thinking about. "They'll kill us if we go home without her, Liam."

"But we're not going to find her!" Liam was practically shouting.

"We might do, we've got to keep looking." And as they turned round a corner Maggie was right there ahead of them, talking to an old man. They couldn't believe their luck. They started yelling and waving their arms at her, and they ran down the street to try to catch up with her.

Maggie had been walking near Leicester Square when she passed the old man sitting on the ground. He was trying to look crippled and get a few coins off people. But it wasn't working so far; he was still stony broke.

Maggie didn't even notice him, she was lost in her own thoughts; she was thinking about going home again. Maybe she'd made a mistake; if she'd said how she'd really felt, maybe she would never have got herself into this mess.

The old man had to call her twice before his voice penetrated her thoughts. He said, "Hey, it's me!

How are you doing? How's young Karen then?"

Maggie turned around. "Oh, it's you!" she said, smiling down.

"Yeah, it's – you're that young Karen's mate aren't you? I've seen you around."

"Yes." Maggie crouched on her heels at the side of the old man.

"How's she doing? She's a good kid, I like Karen."

Maggie sighed. "I don't know," she said. "She got picked up for shop-lifting."

"Oh aye." The old man nodded sombrely. "That's always a danger. Did they let her go afterwards?"

"I don't know," muttered Maggie. "I don't know what happened to her, I can't find her anywhere. I've been looking all over for days now."

"They might put her in a hostel," said the old man, shaking his head at it. "Or put her on probation or – I don't know." He shrugged his shoulders. "How are you doing anyway? Have you found a good kip for the night yet?"

"I've been sleeping in allotments, in one of the huts," she said.

"Not bad, but you've got to be careful," he said. "They don't like you doing that, some folk can turn funny. You'd better clear out right early, before they come."

Maggie nodded. "Yes, I have been doing. I can't get to sleep anyway."

"You look pretty tired."

"Yes, I am," she said.

"It's a pretty tough life. It's a shame about Karen

though, she always seemed to do pretty well at it."

"Yes, I miss her," said Maggie.

"That's the problem with making friends, you miss 'em when they have to go. That's why I'm most generally on my own."

"But you seem to do okay," she said.

"Oh yeah, but I've been around. I wouldn't start on it these days. Not for a million pounds or more."

"How much have you got?" she said.

"You mind your own business!" he said. "About 22p," he added sheepishly.

"Look out!" Gerald just about pulled Liam back from the path of an oncoming goods-wagon. "Are you trying to get killed?" he said.

"We're going to lose her!" said Liam.

"No we're not, just keep shouting! We'll cross the road." They were desperately waiting for a break in the traffic-flow. Maggie couldn't hear them above all the noise it made.

"Here we go!" shouted Gerald and he darted across the road. "Hey, hey, Maggie! Hey, Maggie! It's us, Maggie!"

"Maggie, over here!" yelled Liam, two steps behind him. "Hey, Maggie! Maggie Brady! Over here, Maggie!"

They pushed through the crowd which had suddenly intensified, as though deliberately striving to block their way. "Get out of the way, will you?" Gerald pushed at them desperately. He charged on down the gutter, Liam right behind.

"Hey, hey, Maggie!" They reached the spot where she had been standing.

But she'd gone. The old man sat looking up at them.

"Where'd she go?" Liam pushed past him and ran down the street a short way. "Where'd she go to? Where's she gone?"

"I don't know," said Gerald. He turned to the old man. "Which way did she go, Mister?"

"Which way did who go?" he said, looking ignorant.

"The girl you were talking to!"

"I don't know about that," said the old man, and he sat on the pavement and frowned at them.

"We're her friends!" shouted Liam. "We've been looking all over for her!"

"Aye well, that's as may be. That's what *you* say." The old man gave nothing away, he leaned forward and squinted at them. "Hey, I've seen you before – in the off-licence," he said.

"Never mind that," said Gerald. "Which way did Maggie go?"

"Maggie who?" he said, not willing to help anybody. You never knew what they were up to and he'd learned from experience that all kinds of people wanted all kinds of things. "I don't know no Maggie," he muttered.

"But you were just talking to her!"

"Oh, never mind," muttered Gerald. "We'll find her ourselves."

He ran down the street wildly calling out Maggie's name. But he was heading in entirely the wrong direction.

Chapter Eighteen

The gang met up outside Hanratty's and piled in the back of the Bootes' transit van.

There were six of them altogether, including Alan Foster, who was almost suffocating with tension at the whole affair. He couldn't believe he was in the company of professional criminals! The thought made him dizzy. He couldn't breathe. It didn't even matter that the other youths ignored him, because he was *part* of this, he was part of the Boote brothers' gang!

He was *surrounded* by criminals; they talked of their exploits, building them up to help bring down the tension they felt. They were all feeling nervous, although Alan didn't realize that, he thought it was just him. But setting off on a "job" is like climbing in a boxing ring; you hope you'll win, but you can never be quite certain. You might have trained hard and planned but then so has the other guy; he might land a good one, it might be his night. So you hype yourself up and believe that you cannot lose. But at the back of your mind, there's a tiny doubt.

Which is why they all talked so much. Which is why they all sounded tough. They all had to believe they would win this bout.

Alan didn't say anything though, he was too overwhelmed by it all, and nobody wanted to listen to him anyway. He was just a dumb kid they brought along to make sure no one caught them out. But they were the "real crooks", and he was just chickenfeed.

He kept wanting to ask what it was that they were going to do, but they were talking so much that he couldn't get a word in. Then, as they got closer to the place, they all became silent, and it didn't seem right to start chatting then. So he still didn't know anything when they pulled up outside some flats, and Stevie Boote said, "This is it. Let's get ready, lads."

They were pretty good flats, they were better than where Alan lived; in fact, to his eyes, they were practically *luxury*. Surely they weren't doing a job here near all these *rich* houses? Alan felt out of place, and suddenly it seemed a lot more serious than he had imagined; this was definitely *crime*, it wasn't fooling around.

"Okay, that's the one over there," said Stevie, pointing across the street. "We all go in together and make it quick."

"What do I do?" said Alan.

The other youths sneered at him. "Whaddaya think you do, fat guy? You're the safe-cracker!"

They all fell about laughing and Alan smiled nervously.

"You just stand in the doorway and watch the street." It was Stevie who'd spoken and he took Alan to one side and said, "It's a piece of cake, Alan. Just put this on." He handed Alan a balaclava and Alan started to pull it on. "Not out here, you berk! You wait till we're all inside!"

"Then what do I do?" said Alan.

"You just check no one's coming. And if they do then you whistle."

He put his fingers to his lips and mouthed a whistle.

"I didn't hear anything," said Alan.

Stevie sighed. "I didn't *do* anything! I'm not going to whistle in the street with all the neighbours around! Jeez –" He looked heavenwards and shook his head patiently. "It's a piece of cake. Just do what I told you, right?"

By then the other youths had entered the building and Alan followed on behind feeling miserable. It wasn't what he thought, being part of a criminal gang. He got pushed around as much as he ever did.

He waited in the doorway as Stevie told him to put his hat on, and by this time the others had forced a door. They were bundling inside the first apartment in the corridor. Suddenly this didn't look like much fun at all to Alan. There wasn't any excitement, there was only a fear inside. And the fear suddenly magnified a thousand-fold.

"*Will you watch that street!*" said Stevie. "Don't stare at us, you berk!"

Alan jumped and turned round.

Stevie disappeared.

He seemed to stand for an eternity, feeling small and alone and conspicuous. A lot of responsibility had been placed on his shoulders; he shook as his head tried to cope with it. His face began sweating and streams ran down inside the hat, which was starting to prickle and irritate him. He wanted to rip the thing off and take in great gulps of air. He had the feeling he was about to be suffocated. If they didn't all come back soon he'd probably start to go crazy. He was sorry that Stevie had called round last night.

But he couldn't let them down now and run away, because they would kill him; he was practically sure of that. The Bootes were okay if you kept on the right side of them, but he wouldn't like to see their other side. He'd heard lots of rumours about things they had done to people. He peered over his shoulder – *what was going on?*

There were a lot of loud banging noises coming from the open flat, the kind of noises that someone *had* to hear. They were making so much noise they must have set about wrecking the place. Alan ripped off the balaclava. *What was going on?*

Maybe they'd stepped in an ambush, maybe they were fighting for their lives in there. Maybe he'd better go and see what was going on.

But if he stepped from his post Stevie Boote might well murder him. So he pulled his hat back on, and closed his eyes.

Meanwhile, inside the flat the gang was getting frustrated, they couldn't find the hoard of cash they were looking for. They'd heard that the old man who lived in the apartment kept his loose money handy, and he had plenty loose. He was away at his sister's house and the money should have been easy to find; but they'd checked about everywhere, and drawn a blank.

"Here it is," said Johnny suddenly. He was one of the older members. "It's under the floorboards. Come and give us a hand over here." He started handing bundles of money up; there must have been thousands of pounds, hundreds at least, in big wads.

"Hey, I've got an idea," he said. "Let's wind that thick kid up; let's tell him we came in and topped someone. He's only a kid, and you know what they say about him, he'll probably start blabbing as soon as we get outside. You can't trust a *bird-brain* so let's scare the life out of him. Tell him we killed someone, split some guy's head open."

The other youths grinned at each other; they liked a good wind up. Stevie smiled. "Yeah, it'll help keep his mouth buttoned. Hey, you finished down there?" he said.

"Yeah, I think that's the last of it."

"Right, let's clear off. Let's go and wind Alan up."

"Yeah, but don't do it too soon though, that dumb kid might wet himself. And we're in the back of the van with him!"

"Nah, don't worry," said Stevie. "That Foster kid's *so* dumb he couldn't wet himself unless somebody told him to!"

Alan breathed a sigh of relief as the gang members thundered out of the flat.

"Okay, kid, let's go, don't forget to take your hat off." Someone patted him. "Went like a dream. Like a piece of cake."

They bundled into the van with a clatter of heavy boots. "Has it all gone okay?" said Alan, as he jumped inside.

"Yeah, mostly," said Stevie as he crunched the van into gear. "We had a bit of a problem. How'd it go for you?"

"Okay," said Alan, who was feeling more confident. Maybe that job hadn't been too scary after all. He smiled round the group, but the others were just staring at him. There was a silence as if they were waiting for Stevie to speak.

"Yeah, we had bit of a problem," said Stevie, as they turned into Essex Road. "The old guy was still in there, he was still in bed. We thought he was going away for the week but he musta changed his mind or something. John had to thump him. We think that he croaked the guy."

"Croaked?" Alan said. He wasn't sure that he'd

heard this right. They didn't mean *croaked*, as in "killed", did they?

"Yeah, the guy took a tumble," said Stevie. "Caught his head on the dressing table. He looked like a goner to me, Johnny."

Alan's mouth suddenly dried up. He forced a weak smile to his face. "Are you blokes just winding me up?" he said hopefully.

Stevie shrugged at the wheel. "Wish I was, Al," he murmured, and he caught the boy's eye in the rearview mirror. "We could be up for manslaughter if the old guy don't make it, Al. I think you'd better lie low, and don't say nothing."

"Right," Alan whispered. He could barely get the word out. *Manslaughter.* That was really a big one.

"But maybe he's all right," he said.

"I don't think so, he was spewing blood. For your own sake, Al, don't breathe a word on it."

"But – I wasn't even there," said Alan.

"That don't make no difference, Al. They'll bang you up as well, as an accessory."

"Oh 'eck!" murmured Alan, and the other youths just grinned at him.

Why didn't he just stay at home, like his mother said?

Chapter Nineteen

Patrick Brady was growing desperate; he was having difficulty finding his daughter. She hadn't, as he'd hoped, gone to stay at his sister-in-law's, which meant he had to go looking for her elsewhere. And London was a big place even with all the contacts he had. It could take him a while, and that was dangerous.

He didn't like being out there exposed in this manner, as there was too much risk of the wrong people spotting him. And you couldn't trust everyone to keep their mouths shut about him; the more people he spoke to, so the more was that risk enlarged. He'd already picked up the feeling that someone was following him. He didn't know who, but someone had their eyes on him.

That made Brady nervous; which made him even more dangerous. If he didn't find Maggie soon there'd be trouble ahead . . .

In actual fact the British police were already well aware of Patrick Brady's adventure. They'd known about him since the first day he landed in England. But Brady was posing an unusual problem, and no one was quite sure how to handle it.

They'd had him under surveillance for seventy-two hours, but still no word had come down to arrest the man. This was a puzzle to the officers who were on the surveillance, because Brady was Ireland's most wanted man. It also presented a particular problem to them. The longer they watched Patrick Brady, the more chances that he'd have to spot them, and if he spotted them things might well become violent. If it turned into a shoot-out the public could be at risk, and innocent people might get caught in the crossfire. So they couldn't understand why their superiors dragged their heels. But they didn't know the problems that their superiors faced.

Nobody wanted to make Brady a martyr, and there was a real risk of that happening. He'd come looking for his daughter, a young teenager on the streets – it was bad publicity if this incident was handled in the wrong way.

It could rapidly escalate into an international incident, and if people got hurt it could all backfire. It took only one bullet to land in the wrong place and they would be branded assassins. If they were in

Ireland they would take Brady without a thought. But, in London, they found themselves hamstrung.

So for the time being they settled for keeping close tabs on Brady.

And they wished that his daughter had stayed at home.

Chapter Twenty

Liam and Gerald finally had to acknowledge that they had run out of ideas.

Their spirits had been momentarily lifted when they saw Maggie in the street, but when she vanished their hopes really hit rock bottom. It seemed as though everything conspired to go wrong for them. Not one single break had gone their way.

And now they were tired, they were hungry, their feet hurt and their clothes smelled disgusting. There was no way at all they could see to improve their lot, except by a miracle, and miracles don't grow on trees. But if they continued like this they'd wind up in the gutter. Or even worse; who knows where life might bury them?

So they had to admit that their hopes had turned

cold on them, and then had to decide what to do about it. Which wasn't too easy since their spirits were so low it was hard to string two words together now. Even their thoughts became tired and they had to drag them up from their boots. Their words slurred with the effort of uttering them.

For three days now Liam had been desperately praying that Gerald would finally agree to go home with him. He had always looked up to Gerald, or at least put his faith in him, but he wasn't sure if this was such a good idea any more. Gerald had turned a little crazy. His biggest concern seemed to be what their friends would say if they went home again. But what did that matter? What's the difference if people laughed? It was better than gradually starving to death.

But to Gerald it did matter. He wanted to say to his friends that he was big enough to live in the real world. If they went back home now he would always be stuck there, he would have to work in the factory like the other men.

Liam wasn't concerned about that. He had always been happy there. It was just that Gerald had told him to run away. If only he had just turned his back on him instead of being such a wimp about it. But it was too late for that now. It was much too late.

The biggest problem was that they'd still not found Maggie, and the thought of going home without the girl terrified him. It wasn't just Maggie, but her father was in the IRA. You didn't mess around with those guys, they were dangerous.

"But what shall we do, Gerald?"

"We've got to carry on looking for her." Gerald's mutter was almost inaudible. He kept his head down and kept walking on doggedly, but he was so tired he barely *could* walk now. His vision was blurring, there was a pain in his left leg and another one fixed on his eyebrows. But he had to find Maggie, that's the one thought that drove him on. If they could find Maggie, they could all go back home again.

That's what he hadn't admitted yet, at least not to Liam, that he was as keen as his friend was to go back home. He had tried to be brash about it and keep the game rolling on, but it was no good, he knew they were beaten now. Maybe it wasn't their fault that things hadn't worked out for them, but if they found Maggie they could at least salvage some pride. He could blame it on them and say they whined to come home again, and if it wasn't for that fact he'd have carried on. But the other two got homesick and – yeah, lots of stuff like that. He would be okay then, he could pad it out. It might even look better, it would be like he'd sacrificed something. He had packed up for them – yeah, that's pretty good.

"What are you saying?" said Liam.

Gerald looked up in puzzlement. "I didn't say anything," he said.

"It sounded like you were mumbling something."

"Was I?" Gerald hadn't noticed. All those thoughts must have overflowed. They had better find Maggie soon, he was cracking up.

"You were talking about Maggie."

"Yeah, let's hope we find her soon. She must be scared out of her wits being on her own." And he started to walk faster just to prove that he *wasn't* cracking. But the pace was a strain, and it showed on him.

It was nothing to the strain that was showing on Alan Foster's face as he thought about being hauled up for manslaughter.

Stevie Boote dropped him off about a kilometre from his home, and those five hundred metres were a nightmare. He expected, around every corner, that he would find someone waiting for him; maybe the police, or a jury, or an *executioner*. He couldn't believe he had got himself into such terrible trouble. He couldn't see any way to get out of it.

He couldn't talk to his brothers, they'd probably kill him, and he couldn't talk to his mother – and his dad was gone. He didn't know where his dad was and he couldn't tell him anyway; when it came down to it, he could not tell anyone.

He was shaking with fear and sweat glistened on his face. He looked like he'd just finished running a marathon. He was *really* in trouble. He had better lie low for a while. Then he turned in his street, and he almost screamed.

For in front of the block of flats, right beneath Alan's front window, was a police car with two surly coppers in it. They were checking their notebooks. They were clambering out of the car! They were knocking on *his* door! His heart pounded.

He wasn't to know that they were checking on Billy, who had failed to turn up at his Probation Office. It was just a routine check, the kind of thing they do all the time, but to Alan's mind it was clear: they were looking for him.

So they already knew about it – they must have got a description, maybe someone saw him when he ripped off that stupid hat. Stevie *told* him to put it on, he must have known what he was talking about. And he went and took it off. What a fool he'd been.

And if Stevie found out about it he'd probably murder him! The only job that he'd been on, and they were looking for him. It just wasn't fair, he hadn't even been in the stupid flat! But he'd get the blame for it because somebody saw him. They had his description, and he couldn't drag the others in because if he did they would most likely murder him. They didn't like him much anyway, he could tell how they talked to him. And, besides, they'd just say that it wasn't them. If someone only saw *his* face, the others would say they were somewhere else. It would be his word against theirs – and he knew who'd win.

Oh God, this was terrible, it was getting worse by the moment, and he had no idea at all what to do next. Who did he turn to? Who was going to protect him? He saw no answers so he turned and he ran away. He ran as fast as he could, which was faster than normal, because his legs were scared, too.

The police were out looking for him. They might turn their dogs loose on him. Alan Foster ran like he had never run before.

Chapter Twenty-one

"I've got an idea," said Gerald. "About a place we can stay for a while. Somewhere while we're looking for Maggie."

"Where's that?" Liam wanted to know.

"You're not going to like it much."

Liam stared at him. "Why not?" he said cautiously.

Gerald took a deep breath. "I think we should go back to Murphy's place."

Liam snorted. "Oh sure!" he said sneeringly.

But Gerald had made up his mind, and defended the point. "But what else can we do?" he said. "We've got nowhere else to go. We can go back there and explain to him."

Liam stared in the distance. "He'll kill us," he muttered.

"But why? We didn't do anything to him. I mean, we might have mucked him around but, we'll steal a few things for him and he'll probably let us put up for a while. He's not going to mind as long as he gets something out of it, and in the meantime we can still look for Maggie."

Liam thought over this. He could see that in a strange way it made sense when you actually thought about it. They might even get lucky and get their belongings back. "Do you think he's still got them?" he muttered.

"Got what?"

"Got our bags," said Liam.

"I don't know, I suppose he might have." But they weren't optimistic about it. He didn't look like a bloke to look after things. "We could give it a week," said Gerald, "and if we still haven't found her we could go to a police station and turn it in."

Which was the best news that Liam had had since his spots started clearing up.

He just hoped Murphy wasn't annoyed with them.

Alan Foster ran in absolute terror, without any idea where he was heading for. He had to get help somewhere; he couldn't work this out on his own, but he didn't know who to turn to or where to go.

He couldn't go to his family or talk to his friends about it, in fact his friends would probably laugh at him anyway. They wouldn't believe him and, even if they did, they weren't the kind of people who'd be able to help him. He was starting to see just how poor all his friendships were. There was no one around he could trust. The friends that he hung around with just liked to make fun of him; they were younger than him, he had no friends his own age. He had for a while, but they said he was "mental". They said he was boring. They generally jeered at him.

So now there was no one that he could turn to. Except Stevie – he'd know what he ought to do.

Alan ran round to Stevie's place and banged on the front door, relieved that the white van was parked outside. But when nobody answered for a while he began to get nervous. He could have cried when he heard someone in the hall.

"Who is it?" said Stevie.

"Alan Foster!" he shouted back.

He heard Stevie groan quietly. "What is it now, Alan?" Stevie had been afraid of this, that Alan would start hanging round him now; all because of one lousy job he'd think he was in the gang.

"I've got into trouble! I need some help!" shouted Alan.

"I'm in the bath, Al, can't you come back some other time?" He heard a sigh, then a long pregnant silence. "Oh, hang on a minute, I'll let you come in." The door opened slowly and Stevie stood looking at him with a towel round his waist, dripping water. His long hair hung dark and lank and there were wispy hairs on his chest. "I'm having a bath, couldn't it wait for a while, Alan?"

Alan burst through the door, his face flushed from running hard. "I've just been home, and a police car was waiting there!" He blurted the words out and stood there expectantly, as though Stevie would have all the answers for him.

"So?" Stevie squinted at him, clearly expecting more. "What's the big problem with that, Al?"

"The *police*, Stevie!" Alan stared at him, his eyes almost bulging out. "I mean, that man who died – they've come round to look for me!"

"Oh." Realization suddenly dawned on Stevie Boote. "I see what you mean, Al, looks like you're in trouble. Looks like they've come round to arrest you, eh?" He could hardly believe his luck, the kid fell for it *totally*. He could spin this one out for a good while yet.

"I don't know what to say, Al." He ran a hand through his dripping hair. "But they're quick off the mark, I'll say that for them."

"What do you think I should do?" said Alan.

"I don't know," said Stevie. "We're going to have to think about it. You might have to go on the run for a while."

"Go on the run?" Alan whispered the words out. His heart turned to ice and his breath choked. "Go on the run," he said. "How long do I do that for?"

"I don't know, Al, it kind of depends. You can't show your face around 'cause they've probably got photofits, you'll have to – have you got something fixed up, some place to stay?"

"No." Alan was horrified, he hadn't made *any* arrangements. No one told him that he had to, and he didn't think. But that was what Billy said, "You've

126

got to keep thinking ahead, Alan." Billy always went round to his girlfriend's place.

But Alan didn't have any girlfriends. Alan didn't have *any*one. "Do you think – do you think I'm in trouble then?"

"It looks like it." Stevie sighed heavily. He couldn't believe it, wait till he told them about this one! This daft kid was so dumb it was practically agonising. He shrugged. "I don't know what to say, Alan. You'd best just make a run for it and try to keep out of sight for a while. Keep your head down until it's all over."

"But where will I go?" said Alan.

"You'd better try and find somewhere."

"Couldn't I stay here?"

"No chance, they'll be looking here." Stevie shook his head sombrely. "They'll be looking for you everywhere. You're really in trouble, Al. This time you've really gone and done it."

"But I didn't do anything!" But Alan's protest was a weak one, because he was starting to believe that he actually *had* done something. If they talked it over long enough he would probably convince himself that it was *him* who had murdered the old man.

"It isn't fair," he said miserably.

"But that's how it goes, Al. Look, I'll tell you what I'll do – here's your share of the dough." Alan hadn't even thought about the money; in his fear he'd forgotten that. But Stevie was reaching to the hallstand and taking down his coat.

"You take your share of the dough," he said,

cramming a pile of bank-notes into Alan's hand, "and you hide out, and I'll tell you when the coast is clear."

"Right." Alan bobbed his head eagerly as he stuffed the cash in a pocket. "Thanks a lot, Stevie, you're a really good mate you know."

"Yeah, just you remember that." Stevie opened the front door for him. "So good luck, Al." And he pumped Alan's hand for him.

"Yeah, I was –" But the door had already been closed on him. He really was on his own; he had to go on the run for a while. He didn't know where, but he turned round and trotted off.

Thank heavens for Stevie, he'd have been well stuck without him. Thank heavens that *someone* looked after him.

Murphy just stared as he opened the door on them. "Well, the prodigals return!" he sneered. "Where've you been?"

Liam and Gerald looked at each other, wincing from Murphy's look. "Erm – we've been on the road," said Gerald. "Sleeping rough."

"And now you've come back again to old Uncle Murphy's arms!" Murphy leered at them. "You two are a joke!" he said.

"We were scared about stealing things but – well you tell him, Liam," Gerald nudged his friend painfully in the ribs.

Liam jumped. "Er – that's right, yeah, we think we can do it now. If you're willing, I mean – we'll have a go at it."

Murphy lounged in the doorway carefully studying them, chewing away on a broken match. "Why should I?" he said suddenly, after some time considering it.

"'Cause we'll steal really good stuff!" said Gerald. "We're really determined now, I mean, whatever you want – we can get it for you."

Murphy's expression gave nothing away, he just lounged in the doorway with a sneer on his face. After a minute he leaned to one side to spit a piece of chewed matchstick out, and he grunted a few times as if he was thinking about it.

Finally he turned to look over his shoulder, into the hallway of the house, where he spat again. "I've still got a mattress," he said, with no hint of real friendliness. "But I'm sure enough sick of your playing around."

He turned back and glanced at them. "So you just do it right this time, you boys pay for your way like the rest of us. It won't be like last time, if I think that you're fooling round I'll make damn sure you don't do a runner again."

"Yeah, we will." Gerald breathed with a sigh of relief and his face cheered considerably as he forced a smile. "Have you still got our bags?" he said.

"Are you kidding?" Murphy looked amazed. "Those bags disappeared faster than you two did." He moved to one side to let the two boys walk in again and they returned to the room with the stinking bed.

They threw themselves gratefully at it and thought they'd managed a break at last. And even the smell seemed much better, because they were used to smells.

But the noise hadn't altered, though, the noise of other youths arguing. They fell asleep to the sound of a brawling row.

Chapter Twenty-two

Without any place to go to Alan found himself irresistibly drawn to return to the scene of that morning's crime. It had an effect like a magnet, he couldn't stop thinking about it. He wondered what was going on now the gang had left.

Because he had been part of the gang and he'd left his mark on the place, he wanted to see what it looked like through other eyes. He had become a changed man since this morning. He'd become a man on the run. He was a fugitive.

He arrived at the place in the late afternoon, and peered round cautiously from a bus-shelter at the end of the street. It was even worse than he'd imagined – it seemed that there were police cars all over the place, with blue flashing lights, and loud sirens.

Though in truth most of this was the strain playing tricks on him, because it wasn't that exciting by a long chalk.

There was *one* police car parked there, just doing nothing, and behind that there was one private ambulance. There were also a lot of people standing round which made the whole thing *look* more dramatic. In fact they weren't there to see the place Alan robbed, they were there because an old man had taken a fall. Ambulances attract people, much like fire engines and marching bands. But Alan thought they were there because of the murder – he had it wrong.

In fact, nobody knew that there had been a robbery because the owner was still away. It was in the next flat to his that the man took a fall. Someone had found the man and called for the ambulance, and the police came along as a matter of course. But Alan didn't know that and thought the ambulance was there to take away the murder victim. The police were probably in there now checking out the place for fingerprints. They had already started their enquiries.

Alan began to creep forward, at first almost unnoticeably, with one foot pushed out ahead of the other one. He was moved on inexorably like a fox which smells poisoned bait, and knows that something is wrong, but can't spurn the food. So it was for Alan Foster; the one place he should stay away from was the one place his legs kept him heading for. Moving closer and closer to the edge of the watching crowd, and then further on still, to be part of it.

A stretcher was carried out by two silent men, and

it was clear at this point that the man was dead. There was no doubt about it, the man's eyes were closed and his face white.

Alan's heart started hammering, he could smell the sweat of his own body. He thought that those standing round him would *hear* his guilt. It was screaming out in his mind, it was practically deafening him. Surely they must hear his thoughts, they must know it was him.

But no one turned to look his way, no one seemed to be watching him; he was just one more face in a gawping crowd. As his eyes flickered over them he was almost let down by it. It's not easy to bear such a burden alone.

When he'd stood there for a while, Alan suddenly became aware of a girl who stood right on the edge of the crowd. She hadn't been there before, he was virtually sure of it. It was as if she had suddenly materialized.

There was something different about the girl. Alan couldn't say what it was for a while, but it was as if she was lost in the same way that he was. She was standing apart from things, quietly watching the scene, but not with the same kind of intensity that the others shared. She looked almost bored by it, as though there was nothing else better to do. She looked gentle and calm, a bit like Alan.

He didn't feel gentle and calm then but he was certainly apart from things, and he thought the girl might well share in that loneliness. He was desperate for someone to share his unhappiness, and he was drawn to her as he was to the street itself.

He began edging towards her, trying to think how to talk to her. It was the most tense, awkward moment of his life so far.

Maggie was daydreaming; her thoughts seemed to be miles away. She didn't know what she was thinking of – something about London or the farm back in Ireland or – she couldn't remember.

She was beginning to suffer from the bleak nights and lack of food, and the long days spent trudging around the streets. Now weak in her body, she was *mentally* weaker, too. She was drifting to lassitude. To daydreaming.

She almost jumped as the boy appeared silently alongside her, smiling nervously, awkwardly, *painfully* at her. He seemed almost desperate to find something to say to her. She couldn't think why, she was sure she was nothing much.

"Hi," he said awkwardly, stumbling over the word, though he could hardly have picked a much shorter one. "Do you know what's going on?"

"I think somebody died," she said.

Alan's heart sank. It was true, someone *had* been killed.

"Oh," he said miserably, and his face slumped like wet blancmange. "I thought it was –" he shrugged. "Didn't really know what it was."

Maggie had said it without thinking because she had no idea really, it was just that ambulances and death somehow went together. She didn't really know what had happened, she just stopped to see what was up. It was like reading a poster, or drinking tea. "They're going off now," she said, as the ambulance pulled away. "It's all over now. They're all going away."

Alan was staring at her. She was a terribly attractive girl. He'd never really got close to a girl before.

"What are *you* doing now?" he blurted, practically choking on it, he couldn't *believe* that he was trying to chat her up. In fact, when he thought more about it, it wasn't just chatting up, he had a real need to find someone to talk to. Since he'd been on the run, which he'd been for two hours now, he had felt more utterly alone than ever before.

And this girl didn't laugh at him, or try to make fun of him, she just talked to him as she might talk to anyone. It became suddenly vital that he tried to make friends with this girl.

"I don't know," she said, and it looked as though she meant it, not saying it like some people say it just for acting cool. It really *looked* like she didn't know, like there was no place for her to go. And he was touched by her, he wanted to help her.

"I've got some money," he said, grabbing his pockets, which he hadn't stopped feeling for the last two hours. Ever since he'd been given the money he couldn't believe how much cash there was, he couldn't count it, he was too scared to look at it. There must have been thousands (in fact, there were two hundred pounds); he'd never *had* so much money, never dreamed of it. There seemed such a big hump when he put his hand inside his pocket that he'd had to split it into small piles and spread it around a bit. Someone was certain to see it there, bulging out of his jeans; if he got mugged, at least this way they might miss a bit. There was some in each pocket, there was some tucked into his shoes, he even had some of it balled up in the palm of his hand.

"Do you want to go for a Coke?" he said, quivering with the effort of inviting a strange girl along with him.

"Yes, okay," she murmured.

It was something for her to do. And the boy looked quite nice. His face made her smile.

Chapter Twenty-three

Alan Foster had never realized that you could sit and just talk to a girl before. He thought that all they were interested in was poking their hair around, looking bored and sitting talking to other girls. And the thing that they talked about was the boys who were sitting there, talking about the girls who were sitting there talking about them.

But they never talked about Alan, because Alan didn't count much, he was just there to poke a little bit of fun at. Alan was good for just fooling around with, but to sit and *talk* to him? Girls never did that!

He was almost getting used to it, although he didn't enjoy it much, but he thought that's how it was and would always be. So to find someone who *listened* to him was a whole new experience. He thought for a while he could actually be daydreaming.

And the amazing thing was that she didn't even look *bored* with him; she didn't sit there with her eyes rolling round her head. She didn't stare vaguely in the distance as though she had just spotted Jupiter, or start fingering bruises around her legs.

Alan couldn't get over this; he thought there was something wrong with him. He was so scared he just kept babbling on. And Maggie kept listening as though she found he was interesting; she didn't once force a smirk or bite down a yawn. It was almost unsettling to him, but at the same time it flattered him. He thought he might not be such a great jerk after all.

He couldn't take his eyes off her because she looked such a pretty girl. She was much prettier than all those dumb smirking girls. He found that he was starting to make plans with her and talk about things to do. And the best thing of all, she agreed with him.

He didn't know why, but the answer was plain as day. Because for all that he worried, Maggie *liked* Alan. He was good to just talk to and he didn't put pressure on her.

Alan didn't present any real threat to her.

Evening wore on and they were still in each other's company, although Alan was starting to run out of steam. He'd talked about everything he could think of, but she didn't seem to mind his long silence now. It was pleasant just to walk with him and have someone by her side. After the days spent alone it was comforting.

But Alan was getting worried as night started falling, and this was one of the reasons he'd lost his tongue. He had never stayed away before or spent a night on his own; he was scared of what the darkness might bring. It could be just the first of a long line of lonely nights, with no one he could talk to, and no place to stay. His future looked bleak and he wasn't sure what awaited him. It was a terrible feeling. It was called loneliness.

Conscious then of his own real problems, Alan found himself starting to think about Maggie's home. She hadn't yet mentioned this, though she'd talked about other things, and he wondered how much longer he had with her. The thought of her leaving him made his heart fill with deep despair; it made the long night ahead appear deadening.

So finally he got round to it, and brought the grim subject up. "Where do you live then?" he said, with a sinking feeling.

She shrugged. "I just hang around. I look for a place to sleep, and in the morning I'm back on the street again."

This just about totally floored Alan and he couldn't make sense of it for a while; he thought dossers were old men in dirty coats. He said, "You mean you don't go home and stay with your Mum and Dad? So what do you do? Where do you sleep then?"

"I just kip down anywhere."

"Blimey!" Alan was totally stunned by this. She

sounded so *casual*. "But who wakes you up?" he said. "Where's all your things? I mean, this is – this is totally amazing! You mean that you're sleeping rough?" He was getting excited by it. "So you – what's it all like then? Do you like it?"

"Not much," she said shrugging.

A whole world opened up to Alan; he'd never known a real runaway before. To think that she lived rough and went round just begging things! It was something so different he could hardly get his mind round it, his thoughts were in absolute turmoil. He couldn't believe what a sheltered existence he must have led, he'd learned more in twelve hours than in years before.

"But look – I've got this money," he said. "We could stay in a proper place. If you want to, we could get proper beds for the night."

He came out with this line in absolute innocence, in the way that the idea just came to him. And if he'd said it any other way Maggie probably would have turned him down. But she could see there were no evil thoughts in him.

And the thought *was* appealing, the idea of a comfy bed. She said, "You aren't going to try any funny business?"

Alan was practically mortified. "I was trying to be your friend!" he said.

"Well, okay then. But say you're my brother," she said.

Which is how they began a remarkable friendship. Two young people who were desperate to find some love.

Chapter Twenty-four

Patrick Brady was calling in all of the favours he had ever accumulated, talking to anyone who could help find his step-daughter, and showing her photograph everywhere. He was hoping that someone would have noticed her accent, because accents are a common bond everywhere. He hoped the Irish would stick more or less loosely together, as the British do in places like Hong Kong. He was hoping that somewhere someone Irish had spotted her. She might stick in their minds. He believed she would.

But he spent a day slogging round the city without any real progress, and his tension grew worse as the hours passed. "We're going to have to find her soon," he said, to the man he had brought with him.

"They're still watching us. I can feel it. They're right behind."

The other man said nothing, it wasn't his job to speak. It was his job to protect Patrick Brady.

"It's a dangerous business," muttered Brady. "A dangerous business." And he shook his head and carried on searching.

Gerald and Liam saw her again, and this time they thought they'd caught up with her. They almost whooped with relief as they saw her across the street, with a fat youth, going into a hotel.

They couldn't believe their luck. It was their chance to go home again. They ran like two gusts of wind to catch up with her.

But she had already entered the hotel when they got to it, though it wouldn't matter now, she was still inside. They ran up the stone steps of the small, rather grubby building and banged through the door and stopped at the desk.

Their faces were beaming, they gleamed with excitement. "We've come to see Miss Maggie Brady," Gerald said.

"Who?" The man behind the desk lifted one bushy eyebrow and sneered at them with distaste from beneath it. He didn't like adolescents, especially spotty ones. Especially spotty ones who had filthy clothes on them.

"She's just come in now," said Liam.

"Ah yes, young Miss Brady," he said. He said the words slowly, as though they all tasted bad. He'd had a great many doubts about taking that young couple in, and the only thing that swayed it was that Alan looked old enough. He looked older than he was, otherwise the man would have turned them away. But he'd been having doubts about it ever since.

He didn't mind taking their money but he wasn't too happy about the way they'd spent the whole day in their room watching television. The maid didn't like it either, she said they just stared at her when she went in to clean up and make the beds. There was something not right going on. And now these two spotty youths – well, he thought, this is the end, I'm not having this. He didn't want loads of kids hanging round like the place was a snack bar. These two boys even *smelled*; he was feeling sick.

"Well I can't let you up," he said. "We have to respect our guests' privacy. You'll just have to wait until they decide to come down again."

"Great!" Gerald said happily and flung himself in a chair.

"Not in *here*!" said the man. "Go and wait outside!"

They stood in the street staring up at the hotel, occasionally waving their hands at the windows. They tried a few hopeful shouts but the man put a stop to that. "This place isn't a zoo!" he said furiously.

So now they just waited and lounged round and kicked their heels. They waited an hour, and got bored with it.

"God, I'm starving," said Liam. "We haven't eaten for ages. How much money have you got left in that purse you stole?"

"About £7.50," said Gerald, rifling through it.

"Then why don't we go and get something to eat for a while? There's a cafe there, we could stand here for hours yet –"

So they went to a cafe and ordered lunch. It didn't take too long, but during the time they were in there, Maggie and Alan went on their way.

The man asked them to leave; there was something "not right" about it. And they didn't feel much like arguing, so they went away. They wandered on to another hotel and got a room there for the night.

Liam and Gerald missed them by maybe a minute or so.

Chapter Twenty-five

Patrick Brady called at last on the young man known simply as "Murphy". He greeted him warmly, clasped him by the hand and said, "Hello, Murphy, it's good to meet you finally. You do well on the fund-raising! You're one of the best."

"Ah well, yes, you know how it is – we all do the best that we can, sir." Murphy's face shone delightedly; this was a moment he'd dreamed about, meeting a legend in late Irish history. "It's good to meet you, Mister Brady."

Patrick Brady looked weary. "It's been a long day though, Murphy, do you mind if we sit down and rest a while? I must have walked about half of these streets around London."

"Aye, of course, sir, come on now, we'll sit through

here. Sure there's plenty of streets around here, that's the truth of it!"

"Aye, there are that," said Brady. "It's quite a place." He walked behind Murphy to a quiet, empty room with just a table, a chair and a hook for coats. Murphy checked down the hallway then locked the door carefully.

"Sure, there'll no one disturb us in here," he said. "Can I get something for you?"

"No, I still have some men to see. I've come over here looking for my daughter, Murphy."

"Oh aye?" Murphy's face showed the right concern.

"Aye, she's gone away missing. I don't suppose that you've seen her?" He handed a greatly-creased picture of Maggie across.

"I'm afraid not," said Murphy, after studying the photograph. Though he wished he had, it could do him some good in the world.

"Or what about these two?" said Brady. "They ran away with her." And he handed photographs of Liam and Gerald across.

There was a moment of almost complete disbelief as Murphy studied their faces and slowly grinned. He looked up with a cunning smile and his teeth glittered wickedly. "I think I can help you out there, Mister Brady! Sure, you aren't going to believe what I'm telling you!"

Murphy's laughter rang all round the quiet, empty house, and Patrick Brady just sat looking patiently at him.

It was late by the time Liam and Gerald got back to the squat, having finally found out about Maggie's move. They were not too dejected because they thought they were closer now. They thought the next time they were certain to get to her.

They closed the front door quietly and padded up to their room, and the house seemed strangely quiet all around them. There seemed none of the arguments tearing the evening air, and no one yelled as someone laid a fist to them. It was almost as if they had the house to themselves, which was the first time they'd seen the place empty.

They creaked up the loose floorboards, switched the light on at the top of the stairs, pushed their door open and flung themselves on the bed.

And as they stretched out the door closed and a figure loomed over them.

"I've been looking for you boys," smiled Brady.

They both froze. They were horrified. Patrick Brady almost filled the room, he was like the Rock of Gibraltar towering over them. His face appeared to be deadly calm but his voice was a rumbling wave. "I've come a long way to find what you took from me."

"No! We didn't take her!" said Gerald. "She wanted to come away! We just –" He closed his mouth. It was no time to start to blab. Patrick Brady didn't want blabbing, he wanted some answers. And the boys didn't have them to give to him.

Patrick Brady kept smiling at him, with a strange, almost wistful smile. "Where is she then, Gerald? Where's Maggie?"

"We don't know," croaked Gerald, with a dry feeling in his throat. "She's with a boy. She moved out of her hotel."

"And where did she go?" said Brady.

Liam and Gerald just looked at each other.

"We don't know," they said, flinching in unison.

Patrick Brady's face changed. A dark look slid across his mouth, a dark look like a thundercloud brewing up. "You've got no idea?" he said.

Gerald looked around desperately, looking for something to help them get out of this. "She knows an old man!" he said. He was clutching at straws, he was trying to prevent the inevitable. "We've seen Maggie talking to him. *He'll* know where Maggie's gone." He might *not* know, but at least it would gain some time. "You see him hanging round Piccadilly."

"What does this old man look like?"

"Just an old man, like a tramp, he's dead easy to spot. He's always round Piccadilly – isn't that so, Liam?"

But Liam was unable to actually say anything. Liam believed Patrick Brady would *murder* him.

"All right, show me," said Brady suddenly, as he dragged the boys to their feet. "And for your sake just hope that we find this man."

"Oh we will!" shouted Gerald. "We'll find him dead easy!"

He just hoped that the old man could tell them something.

Chapter Twenty-six

The two boys lay quietly in a hospital side-ward wondering if they might yet be able to count all their blessings up. They had survived Patrick Brady's rage; they had been knocked about a bit, but on the whole they were just badly shaken up.

They didn't yet know what was going to happen to them, but they wanted to stay in the room as long as possible. They were safe and protected there, they were fed and looked after, if they hadn't been so scared they'd have worshipped it.

It was morning, and bright sunlight fell through a window on the bed where Liam counted his bruises. Gerald was looking at him. He had already counted his. He was surprised there were less than he thought there were. He had the feeling he might look a bit like a plum pudding, but he told himself to treat them as battle-scars.

He looked around nervously as the door opened on them and a group of men filed in the little room. All his tension returned again. He was filled with uncertainty. These days every new turn could prove worrying.

One of the men smiled at him. "Hello lads, how are you feeling today?"

"Not too bad," murmured Gerald. "A bit stiff, you know."

The man nodded encouragingly. "That's good, you had quite a scare. Patrick Brady's not a man to get mad at you."

You can say that again, thought Gerald.

"My name is Inspector Reece. I'm the investigating police officer."

Liam looked up. Now the police. That was all they needed!

"We're interested in finding out Maggie Brady's whereabouts. I assume that's why Patrick Brady called on you."

"But we couldn't tell him nothing," said Gerald, and his lips started quivering. The emotion was all building up in him. "We didn't know where she was, we've been looking all over for her. We thought we found where she was – but she moved away."

He let his head hang pathetically as the detective sat down by him. "It's okay, son, just tell us what you know."

Gerald looked up and sniffed and tried blinking

some tears away. "We kept looking for her, but we couldn't find her anywhere." His voice came in gulps, he had to keep stopping to wipe his nose. "And we kept finding her, and she kept going away again. We wanted to go back home but we needed to take her with us, and then –"

"Where is she now?" said Inspector Reece.

"I don't know," sobbed Gerald. "We tried looking everywhere. But she just disappeared. We looked everywhere!" He looked up at the detective through a bright film of tears, and his body shook as he tried not to cry.

The detective was nodding at him, trying to encourage him. "It's okay," he said quietly. "Just carry on."

"Well –" Gerald sniffed noisily. "And then Mister Brady came, and we couldn't tell him anything either. Except about the old man and I was really just making that up. Then he got pretty mad – and he battered us."

"Did he hurt you?" asked Inspector Reece.

"He mostly just threatened us. It was the old man who came in for the worst of it." He shook his head sadly. "I didn't think that would happen. I mean, I didn't want the old man to get beaten up."

"No, he'll be okay," said the detective. "He's in another hospital. Do you think that he knows? The old man I mean."

"I don't know," Gerald bleated. "He might do. We just said it to get Mister Brady away, do you know what I mean?" He raised his head helplessly and this

151

time the tears were falling. He could hardly see anything through all the tears.

Inspector Reece gave his nod again and looked at his colleagues who'd been standing there throughout, simply listening.

"What's going to happen to us now?" said Gerald.

"We're going to send you back home again."

"Back to Ireland?" Gerald's face barely dared to hope.

"Unless you want to stay here," said the Inspector. "But you're better off at home, I think. Just relax, you'll be home in a day or two."

On the other bed Liam felt the tears trickle down his cheeks. He had never felt such a relief before.

In a hospital two miles away the old man was lying with his eyes closed, and it looked as though he'd been through a hard time. His face was all puffed up and there were angry cuts round his mouth, and his left eye was closed by a savage bruise. He was breathing irregularly, but his condition wasn't serious. When he healed up he'd be right as rain again.

He opened his one useful eye as the detectives stepped in the room and said, "I didn't tell 'em nothing!" Then he closed his eye.

"They tried beatin' it out of me," he said in the barest of whispers. "And I could have told 'em, but I didn't say nothing."

"So where is she now?" asked Reece, but the old man didn't seem to hear.

"Didn't tell 'em one single thing," he said bitterly.

"Do you know where she is now?"

The old man's head rolled upon the pillow and he looked to be sleeping, but then he spoke again. "No, I'd never give her away," he said. "She's a nice girl, and so was Karen. I saw her yesterday with that young lad she's got in tow. I said, 'Who's that? Is this your new boyfriend?' and she really laughed. Yeah, we had a few laughs together, me and her. You know, she always had words for me. Never just passed me by. No, I wouldn't tell them buggers *anything*. I tried fighting 'em back but they were too big and strong for me. I'm just getting too old, I can't take it no more."

And he lay breathing noisily with a film of sweat covering his face.

"Where is she now, Tom?"

"She's at that new Prince Hotel."

Chapter Twenty-seven

But they'd left the Prince Hotel now, as they moved on from everywhere when the management became uneasy about having them there. It was becoming a joke to them, they felt like unwanted guests turning up in the middle of a Sunday tea. They were getting hysterical at the faces the people wore. They were having the times of their lives with it.

They were staying at that moment in a small detached boarding house where a landlady had finally taken pity on them. It was getting late when they called, and though she didn't like having them there it was better than thinking of them walking the streets alone. They were too young for that, she could tell just by looking at them. So she gave a long sigh. "You can stay," she said.

When they were settled in their room Maggie started to talk about something that had been bothering her for a while now – their cash supply. It was running out fast, they could see the end coming now. They had to make some decisions. It was time to talk.

"I think I'm going to go home, Alan," she said.

He nodded. "Yeah, I think I will too. I'll go and talk to me mum about it, she'll know what to do. And this anorak needs fixing – the zip's come undone. Me mum's good at things like that. So I think I'll go home again. When the money's run out, do you think we should go home then?" He looked up at Maggie and stared at her face for a while, because they were talking about splitting up, which wasn't easy. She would leave a big hole in his life, he would never be quite the same. But he'd grown up, and knew this time had an end to it.

It was desperately hard though, he was going to miss her. It was hard to try even considering it. But they'd left different worlds behind and they were two different people. It was time to go back to their families.

"Yes, I'm going to talk to my dad," she said, looking away from him, because she felt just the same and it saddened her. "But we've had lots of fun!" she laughed.

"Yeah, we sure have, we've had a laugh! But – I'm really going to miss you, you know, Maggie."

"I'll miss you too, Alan."

"Yeah." He looked away in embarrassment and

toyed with the zip of his anorak. "Maybe I'll come over and see you," he said.

"Yeah you must, that would be really great! I could show you all over! We could –" but her voice had already grown small in her. Her thoughts had already turned back to being in Ireland. She was missing it. She was missing her stepfather.

She didn't think that she would but she couldn't hide the truth from herself; no matter what she thought at the time, she still loved the man. She hadn't ever realized that, it must have crept up unnoticed on her. But she missed having Patrick around the place. She missed his kindness and laughter and how he stopped the boys teasing her. That's what made it all so confusing. For how could he be like that when he was a chief in the IRA? She wanted to ask him about it and see what he said.

And perhaps she could explain to him that there are better ways of doing things – she'd seen that herself in the last few days. They didn't have to be criminals hiding out on some lonely farm. They could try to live like any normal family.

She knew it wouldn't be easy because he had different dreams from hers, but she thought he ought to try telling her his side of it. And if she didn't like it she could just walk away again. There was nothing to stop her, she'd done it now.

So she'd reached a decision that it was time to go home again. To have it out with him. To take on the IRA.

"Maggie?" said Alan. "I'm starting to get hungry.

Should we go and get something to eat do you think?"

Maggie nodded her agreement.

"There's a cafe just over there."

So they went out for one final meal together.

The cafe was situated on the far side of some rough waste ground, and they had to pick their way over it, dodging bricks. It was reaching late evening and the sky bruised like ripened fruit. A cool wind blew across them, refreshing them.

Maggie said, "I've had a really good time, Alan. It's the best time I've ever had. I'm going to miss you. I really will miss you, Alan."

But Alan didn't say anything because he was already missing her. It was the hardest thing he'd ever had to feel.

"We might meet again," she said.

He nodded. "We might," he said, and then he remembered that he'd left something in the room. He had to go back for it, which is when things caught up with them. And after that nothing would ever be quite the same.

For Patrick Brady had been tracking them with the aid of a trade directory, working his way through every hotel they might have stayed at. And now he'd located them, just as Alan turned towards the house.

And so had Connor Cole – the assassin.

Chapter Twenty-eight

Maggie stood waiting for Alan to return with the breeze playing games with her tousled hair. She was drawing with her foot on the dry, dusty ground, and thinking about going back to Ireland. Now that she'd decided there was no point in putting it off, she should make her way as soon as possible. She could find Aunty Jean's place and borrow some money from her, enough for the ferry and a train back to Dublin. After that she could walk, or could phone from the station. She could be home by the end of the week maybe.

She was working on the final few details she needed when she heard someone coming and turned around.

"Is that you, Alan?" she said, but she knew that it

wasn't him, she could tell by the sound that the footsteps made. They were heavier than Alan's, they were walking more slowly. Maggie stiffened. She said again, "Is that you, Alan?"

Someone was walking towards her with their shape silhouetted by the light of a flickering streetlamp. She peered closer – she recognized it, the shape that was looming up. She said, "Daddy? Is that you? Is that you, Daddy?"

Maggie couldn't believe it. She took a cautious step forward.

"Is it you?"

The feet stopped. "Aye, it's me, Maggie."

"Oh – oh, Daddy." Her voice trembled. She couldn't believe it, that he'd come over here just to look for her. He had travelled to England, the place of his greatest fear. A sudden lump filled her throat, her sight swirled for a minute.

Patrick Brady's voice came again, soft as a summer breeze. He said, "Maggie, I've been looking all over for you. Are you all right, Maggie? I've been so worried about you."

"Yes, I'm fine," she said, scarcely even whispering.

He was about twenty-five metres away when he suddenly halted, as if awaiting her permission to come close to her. "I've been so worried, Maggie," he whispered. "I don't know what I've done wrong – but I love you – I want you back home again." He could hardly get his words out, there were tears mixed up with his voice, and suddenly Maggie was running, and she practically dived at him.

"Oh Daddy!" she gasped as his arms almost crushed her breath. "Oh Daddy, I'm so sorry I ran away!"

But he said, "No, it's me, Maggie. I'm sorry too, Maggie." And he held her as though they would never part.

And they held that embrace for what seemed like eternity, for there was no more to say and no voice to speak. But it was only a minute when a voice from the darkness said, "Well now, isn't that sweet? What a pretty scene!"

Patrick Brady whirled suddenly, with Maggie clasped to his breast. "Who's that there?" he said angrily. "Show yourself!"

And he growled as a figure stepped from the encircling darkness with the ease of a cat stalking its prey. "So you've found her at last, Patrick. I was hoping you wouldn't, really. I was hoping it wouldn't have to end this way."

"Who are you?" said Brady, with a sudden, cold shock like the blade of a knife pressed against his neck.

"Don't you know me then, Patrick?"

"Well how could I know you? I can't see you, you're standing right in the shade!"

"Then I'll move to the light," said the man, and he took a step sideways.

"Who is it, Daddy?" said Maggie, in Brady's arms.

He didn't answer for a moment. Then he said, "Connor Cole."

"Aye, it's I," Connor Cole said, with the faintest of

smiles. "With one last job to do. One commission left."

"What do you mean?" muttered Brady.

"I think you know that already. Ireland does need its heroes and its dead, Patrick."

Patrick Brady was silent. Then he said, "Not the child, Connor – for God's sake, have you got no *heart* in you? We'll be back on the farm tomorrow! There's no need for this!"

But Connor Cole shook his head. "Yes there is, Patrick. We'll have one more dead hero, gunned down by the British. You will live on for ever. You'll never die."

"But let the girl go, Connor –"

"I did think of that, Patrick." Connor Cole shook his head, as if in remorse. "But it wouldn't quite work, would it? The girl's seen my face, Patrick. She could tell what's gone on. Tell the truth, Patrick. And we don't want the truth, we want lies we can build upon. You know all about lies, that's your job, Patrick."

"You're a cold-hearted swine," said Brady. "That's what they call you!"

"Aye, they could be right there," Cole said nonchalantly. He looked down at his side, where a gun was pressed to his coat. "You know – this isn't a personal thing, Patrick." He looked up and right at Brady. "I've got nothing against you. But it's the business we're in. It's *my* job, Patrick."

"Aye, I know," muttered Brady. "You're the

worst kind of man, Connor Cole. Killing for cash, with no soul at all."

"Is he going to kill us?" whispered Maggie.

"No, child." Brady's hand moved to cover her eyes. "We'll go home very shortly, so be brave, Maggie."

And his body tried to shield her as Cole raised the gun into view.

"I shall see you in hell, Connor Cole!" he swore.

Chapter Twenty-nine

Detectives had been watching the scene. Some had followed Patrick Brady; some, like Brady, had been checking hotels to see if they could locate his daughter. They were puzzled when Cole made his appearance.

"Who do you think that is?" said one of the detectives, who was sharing a car with Inspector Reece.

Inspector Reece shrugged. "Search me," he murmured. "Another one of his contacts most probably."

"Should we pick him up now? I mean, now he's found his daughter."

Inspector Reece shrugged again. "I don't know," he said.

The detective was puzzled. "What do you mean, you don't know?"

"I mean nobody's told me what to do yet!" The Inspector was irritated and it showed in his manner. He didn't like hanging around waiting for orders. He wanted to pick Brady up or forget the whole business, simply watching him was a pain in the backside. He sighed. "Oh, I'm bored to death. Let's hope he goes home soon. At least he'll be somebody else's problem."

"What's that in his hand?" said the other man.

"Which hand?" The Inspector leaned forward, trying to peer through the gloom of the thickening night.

"The new man, he's holding something down by his side."

Inspector Reece squinted.

"He's holding a gun!" he said. He grabbed for the radio and shouted a quick command.

"One of the suspects is armed! Let's move carefully!"

Alan Foster's mind was idling miles away as he jogged along trying to catch Maggie up. He wasn't making much speed on the dark, rather tricky ground, which was littered with rubble and willow herb. It sounded as though he was grunting but he was murmuring his thoughts aloud, a habit he had had since he learned to talk. And he was waving his arms about to try to ward off the willow herb, and he almost ran straight into Connor Cole.

The scene made him jerk to a stop. He couldn't quite make it out, except someone had Maggie, and was threatening her. One held a gun on her while another man was wrestling her – he was a big man, so big that she couldn't fight.

"Maggie!" he cried, and went rushing forward, although the odds against winning were pretty slim. He was only a boy against two hefty armed men; but in that moment he didn't stop to think about it. All he knew was that he had to defend Maggie. If it meant getting hurt, that was the price he paid.

Connor Cole saw him as he half-turned around, but he was just a low blur in the corner of his eye, just a form in the darkness which made for him.

"Run, Maggie, run!" yelled Alan, as he headed straight for the man.

And Connor Cole squeezed the trigger instinctively.

"Oof!" Alan flew back in a welter of arms and legs as a bullet tore his shoulder and threw him flat.

He tried to climb to his feet and then realized that he'd been shot. "He's got a gun, Maggie, run! Maggie, get away!"

Alan tried to stand up again and there was a pain searing down his arm. He felt giddy, and the night did a cartwheel. He got as far as his knees and tried scrambling forward, but then pitched in the long grass and gave a cry.

"Oh Maggie run, run away!" he cried, but his voice was too weak for him, nothing came out but the barest sigh. And it seemed nobody heard it as he rolled slowly on his back, and stared up at the sky and the twinkling stars.

The detectives, still in the process of closing in, froze at the sound of the gunshot.

"He's just gone and shot someone!"

"It's a kid! He just shot some kid!"

The Inspector couldn't wait any longer. That was the decider; they couldn't hang around for ever while some bloke in an office thought of what to do. He pulled out his own gun.

"You're surrounded by police officers! Put the gun down and back away slowly! Put your hands behind your head. And you too, Mister Brady! Kneel on the ground, and then spread yourself face down!"

Patrick Brady just stared at Cole. "What's it going to be now, Connor?"

Connor Cole kept the gun on him while he worked it out. His eyes darted round the scene. There were policemen coming from all angles.

He said, "It looks like it's over," and dropped the gun. He let it fall to the ground and took a careful step backwards. And then he knelt down and laid himself on the ground.

Inspector Reece hurried past him and knelt by the bleeding boy.

"It's okay now, you're going to be all right," he said. He took a look at the wound. "*Will you get someone over here*! And get an ambulance to come down immediately!"

Alan opened his eyes. "He just shot me!" he whimpered.

"It's okay, it's only a shoulder wound. You're not going to die, it's only a shoulder wound. Just lie here, we'll get someone down to you." He took off his jacket and arranged it across the boy. "There'll be an ambulance here soon, just relax, sonny."

And while he was talking, Maggie tore out of Brady's arms and screamed, "Alan!" and sprinted across to him. She flung herself to the ground, but was frightened to touch the boy. "Is he going to be all right?" she said desperately.

"Yes, he should be all right," said Reece. "Though he won't do the pole vault for a while. You'd better sit with him while I try to sort this lot out. And try not to move him, I'll send someone over to you." And he looked around. "*Will you get someone over here!*"

Chapter Thirty

Patrick Brady stood quietly with Inspector Reece while the confusion slowly settled before them. Connor Cole had been quickly searched, his hands cuffed behind his back, and was being led towards one of the police cars. An ambulance had turned up, and a woman with a stretcher was bending down checking on Alan's wound.

The detectives stood around Alan trying to take down his details, but Alan's thoughts were all pointing at Maggie. Despite all the pain he had, he had the unhappy feeling that this was the last time he would ever see Maggie. So he wanted to make it last, so he'd always remember her. Next to that, the pain seemed quite a minor thing.

The two men standing watching hadn't said a great

deal to each other, but a strange understanding grew between them. It was as if they were old friends, not longstanding enemies. All the tension had cut through their differences.

"That boy probably saved your life, Brady," said Reece.

"Aye, I know that," Brady murmured softly. "He did it for Maggie, trying to save her. He's a hell of a lad, he's loaded with guts all right."

The Inspector stared at Alan. "But it wasn't just guts," he said. "He did it through love. You could try to consider that. Maybe you can learn something, Brady."

Patrick Brady nodded slowly. "I already have," he sighed. "I've already learned a great many things." He was watching his daughter as she stood close by Alan's side. "So what happens now?" he said cautiously.

"It's been left up to me," said Reece. "Left to my 'discretion'. Which means nobody else wants to take the responsibility."

Patrick Brady nodded slowly. "And what does your discretion tell you?"

"That I should lock you up and throw the damn key away," said Reece. "But that wouldn't help your daughter much, would it? It's time to remember that it's sometimes the children who pay for the sins of their fathers."

"Aye," muttered Brady. "Sometimes we forget that."

Inspector Reece cleared his throat. "So here's

what we're going to do. I'm going to drive you to Liverpool. You'll get an escort right to the ferry. Then you take your daughter home and never come back again. I don't want to see children get caught in the crossfire."

"Nor do I," murmured Brady. "Nor do I, Inspector."

The Inspector moved away then as Alan was lifted gingerly on to the stretcher. He stood at Alan's side and said a few words to him. "You're going to be all right, Alan, you're a pretty tough customer."

"Yeah." Alan blushed with a flood of embarrassment. "But what about Maggie?" he said.

The Inspector turned round and cast a long look at her. "I'm afraid that she has to go home, Alan."

"I was afraid of that happening. Do you think that I might ever see her again?"

"I don't know, Alan. But I don't think it's likely." He put a hand on his arm. "It's just the way that it is, Alan. I'm sorry." Then he turned round and walked away.

He walked up to Maggie and said, "Come on, love, it's time to go."

"Time to go home?" said Maggie.

"Time to go home," he said.

"I had a friend who's called Karen," she said. "But I think she was arrested."

"Was she a runaway? I'll try to find out about her."

"Could you write and tell me?"

"I don't think I can do that, Maggie. But I'll give

you a phone number where you can contact me. If you call me in a couple of weeks I'll see if I can find out something –"

Maggie stopped. "Is he going to be all right?" she said.

"Alan? He'll be fine."

"He's a –" She couldn't find the words for it.

But he knew what she meant. "Yes he is," he said.

MYSTERY THRILLER

Introducing, a new series of hard hitting, action packed thrillers for young adults.

THE SONG OF THE DEAD by Anthony Masters

For the first time in years 'the song of the dead' is heard around the mud flats of Whitstable. But this time is it really the ghostly cries of dead sailors? Or is it something far more sinister? Barney Hampton is sure that something strange is going on – and he's determined to get to the bottom of the mystery . . .

THE FERRYMAN'S SON by Ian Strachan

Rob is convinced that Drewe and Miles are up to no good. Why else would two sleek city whizz-kids want to spend the summer yachting around a sleepy Devonshire village? Where do they go on their frequent night cruises? And why does the lovely Kimberley go with them? Then Kimberley disappears, and Rob finds himself embroiled in a web of deadly intrigue . . .

Further titles to look out for in the Mystery Thriller series:

Treasure of Grey Manor by Terry Deary
The Foggiest by Dave Belbin
Blue Murder by Jay Kelso
Dead Man's Secret by Linda Allen